CW00520106

A
Country
Practice

To Everything a Season

JUDITH COLQUHOUN

A Country Practice © JNP Films Pty Ltd
This novelization © Judith Colquhoun (2015) is based on 'A
Country Practice' stories from the initial television series

Published 2015 by Corazon Books
(Wyndham Media Ltd)
27, Old Gloucester Street, London WC1N 3AX
www.greatstorieswithheart.com

The author has asserted her right to be identified as the author
of this work in accordance with the Copyright, Designs and
Patents Act 1988.

This book is a work of fiction. The names, characters,
organisations and events are a product of the author's
imagination and any resemblance to actual persons, living or
dead, organisations and events is purely coincidental.

All rights reserved. No part of this publication may be
reproduced or transmitted in any form or by any means,
electronic, mechanical, or otherwise, without the prior
permission of the publisher.

ISBN-13: 978-1909752221
ISBN-10: 1909752223

Also in the A Country Practice series
A Country Practice Book 1: New Beginnings

Coming in 2016
A Country Practice Book 3

Read more about the series at
www.acountrypractice.info

CHAPTER ONE

The long, hot summer was over and autumn had come at last to Wandin Valley. Golden willows lined the creeks; in the paddocks, dotted amongst the ubiquitous gums, the reds and yellows of oak and elm and chestnut glowed brightly, while all along Mrs Harriet Eldershaw's drive, her beeches blazed like a bushfire. You had to give it to the early settlers, their nostalgia for distant climes had improved the landscape considerably – that is, if one overlooked the undergrowth, choked as it so often was with hawthorn and blackberries and Paterson's Curse.

Terence Elliot was admiring the beeches now from Harriet's shaded verandah where the two of them were having afternoon tea. The pot was silver, the scones were delicious, the sponge cake perfection. Were it not for the aforementioned gumtrees, and the rows of grapevines marching away in ordered rows before him, Terence felt he could have been at some English country house, albeit one in need of some repair. The effect was heightened every time Harriet spoke, for although she'd been in Victoria for nearly half a century, she had never quite lost those Home County vowels. Terence had known her for some time, though they weren't close – she was far too healthy to often require the services of a doctor. He wished he'd had the chance to gain her friendship.

'I'm glad autumn's come at last,' Harriet said. 'I wanted to see my beech trees in all their glory one last time.' She smiled. 'Your beech trees now.'

'Let's share them, shall we?' said Terence. 'You know you'll be welcome to visit any time. And they're not really mine for another month.'

'That's what I wanted to talk to you about, Terence. The packers are coming in two days, I'm putting everything into storage and I'm taking off. I've booked a flight to England and I don't know when I'll be back.'

'You've still got family there?'

'A sister and several cousins. I haven't seen them for ten years.'

'Then it's time you went.'

'The thing is, the grapes are the best they've been for years – someone should keep an eye on them until vintage. Someone besides the silvereyes, that is, the wretched creatures have already had more than their fair share.'

'Those beautiful fake owls you've got don't work then?'

'A minor deterrent only. You should think about netting next year, it's really the only solution but it is hard work. Anyway, I thought perhaps we could come to some arrangement … you pay a peppercorn rent until settlement and take over straight away. What do you think?'

'That you're a far-sighted and generous woman, Harriet.'

'I can't abide waste. You agree then?'

'I do. Though I can't guarantee I'll be able to make

wine this year. I've got a lot to learn.'

'Sell the grapes to Ian Jamieson, he makes a decent cabernet. And he'll pay you in kind if you like.'

'Sounds like a win-win.'

'For all of us. I'm so glad you bought this place. I know it needs a lot of work and people will no doubt tell you you're quite mad to take it on but I'm sure that in time you'll bring it back to its former glory.'

'I'll certainly do my best, Harriet.'

'And you'll succeed. You'll fall in love with the place, as I did all those years ago. A moment.' She disappeared through the French doors and returned with a small tray holding an old bottle and two small crystal glasses. She uncorked the bottle and poured the amber liquid.

'Lester's last tokay.' She passed one to Terence. 'Shall we drink a toast, then? New beginnings for both of us.'

'To new beginnings.'

The tokay was delicious, smooth and mellow. Terence hoped it was a harbinger of things to come. He hoped that Harriet's trip back to the land of her birth would bring her much pleasure. And he hoped that he himself was not indeed quite mad in taking on this lovely but very rundown old vineyard.

While the grapes were not yet ready to be picked, Wandin Valley was gearing itself up for the apple harvest. This annual event divided the town into two camps. There were those who regarded it as a blessing – mainly, it must be said, on economic grounds. On the other side were those who – lacking a certain tolerance – would have all the pickers arrested on sight. Even while Terence Elliot was enjoying his tea with Harriet Eldershaw, the matter was being rehashed in the local post office. Esme Watson had the floor. Esme, it transpired, had passed a broken-down car on her way back from Burrigan and had failed to stop and render assistance.

'I'm sure I know my Christian duty,' she said, 'but really, I was just too frightened to stop. If I'd had someone with me, then maybe – but I was all alone. A single woman. What if they'd attacked me?'

'*Attacked* you, Miss Watson?' Molly Jones sounded as though she could hardly imagine anything less probable.

'There were three of them, Molly. Three pickers. Well, two I suppose. One was a child.'

'And this child was going to attack you if you stopped to offer help?'

'They looked like gypsies. They can't be trusted. That's all I'm saying.'

Molly rolled her eyes and paid for her stamps. 'I'm sure the pickers bring quite a bit of money to the town, don't they?' she asked innocently.

'They do indeed,' said Ida Dugdale, the postmistress, who was very much in favour of the itinerants. 'Don't do you any harm either, do they, Andy?' Andy Mackay owned the local bakery. His pies were legendary. He smiled agreement.

'My profits go up by fifteen percent.'

'There are more important things than money!' snapped Esme. 'You ask Sergeant Gilroy how he feels about this – this invasion. About the increase in crime! You just wait until some defenceless woman is violated in her bed!' And much put out, Miss Watson left.

'Poor love,' Molly said, not entirely without sympathy. 'She seems to have an absolute thing about the pickers, doesn't she? I wonder why?'

Liz Anderson, the principal of the local primary school, decided it was time to have her say. 'Well it's not their fault, but they do cause a huge problem for the school.'

'How, Liz? What do they do?' Andy asked.

Liz laughed. 'They turn up! Or the kids do. You said your profits go up by fifteen percent, Andy – well so do my class sizes. Trouble is, we don't get any extra funding so I can't employ another teacher. As well as that, the kids are from all over, from interstate, they're all at different levels – it's challenging, to say the least. But we've just got to make the best of it – the fruit has to be picked.'

'Either that or we leave it to the cockatoos,' said Andy. 'I swear I've never seen such big flocks of them. Biding their time, just waiting to swoop.'

'Tell me about it,' Molly sighed. 'They got all our plums, left me just enough for two small jars of jam. I'm for the pickers, they can be my avenging angels.'

A huge flock of those very cockatoos rose screeching from the nearby paddock as Bill Ferguson pulled his ute off the road. A battered old station-wagon had broken down; an elderly man, a young woman and a small boy stood beside it. They did not look like avenging angels. Poor sods, thought Bill and went to see if he could lend a hand. Unlike Esme Watson, Bill did not see every fruit-picker as a potential serial killer.

'G'day,' he said. 'What seems to be the trouble?'

The man came forward to meet him. 'Thank you so much for stopping. It is, I think, old age. Mine, that is. We have a flat tyre but I cannot get the nuts off to remove it.'

Bill sensed the old man's discomfort in asking for help, or appearing vulnerable. He had quite a strong accent, middle European maybe, but his English was good, his manner self-deprecating. The woman seemed wary, she kept an arm around the child and watched intently. Bill smiled in sympathy, trying to put them all at ease.

'Like me to have a go?' he said. 'They can be a bugger sometimes. Oh, I'm Bill, by the way. Bill Ferguson. Got a farm up the road a bit.'

'Alex Popovich,' the old man said. 'This is my daughter-in-law … my grandson.' But he did not give their names. He handed Bill the shifter and took him round to the passenger side. It was the rear wheel. The jack looked even older than the car and not fit to bear its weight. Bill was glad that he did not need to get underneath. The nuts were indeed tight and it took all his strength to get them off but eventually the job was done and the tyre, which was badly damaged, came off. Alex Popovich had the spare out, waiting. It was not, Bill noticed, in very good shape.

'Where are you going to be picking?' he asked as he got it into position.

'Cameron's,' said Popovich.

'Oh yeah,' said Bill, non-committal but thinking, God help them. 'Been there before?' Popovich just nodded.

'I guess you don't get much say,' Bill said.

'You do not. But the boss – I mean the gang boss – he is a good man.'

'Well I suppose that counts for a lot. There you go, then.' He was about to leave it at that, he'd done his good deed, he thought he should probably go and let these people get on with their lives. But he could feel the little boy staring at him, he knew the child had watched his every move. He sensed too that this little family had known better times, they had not always had to drive a beaten-up Holden from job to job.

'Tell you what,' Bill said. 'I used to have a wagon like this. Sold her a while back. But I reckon I've still got a couple of decent tyres. And you're going to need a new spare. I'll hunt them out, bring one out to you.'

Finally the young woman spoke up. 'We couldn't let you do that. Could we, Dad?'

But Alex didn't get a chance to speak. 'Just cluttering the place up,' Bill said. He smiled again, a slow, conspiratorial smile. 'Hey, I reckon anyone brave enough to work for Bruce Cameron deserves a break. See you in a day or two.' He ambled back to his ute, gave them a wave and drove off. The little boy looked after him, awestruck, waving back till he was out of sight.

'Do you reckon he meant it?' the woman, Silvia, said.

Alex just shrugged. A long hard life had taught him not to count on anything. 'We'd better get going, we don't want Robbo to think we are not coming.'

They arrived at Bruce Cameron's orchard half an hour later. Cameron was talking to Robbo, who had hired the gang of pickers as he did every year. Alex got out of the car to report their arrival. Robbo greeted him warmly; not so Bruce Cameron.

'Not you again,' was what he said. He turned to Robbo. 'You never mentioned the Popoviches.'

'On the list, Bruce. Good workers, too.'

'You reckon?'

Robbo gave him a long look, daring him to make an issue of it. 'Can we just see how it goes?'

'Got to fill their quota like everyone else,' Cameron said and he walked off.

'We won't let you down, Robbo.'

'I know, mate. Staying at the camp park?' Alex nodded. Robbo went with him back to the wagon and stuck his head in the window to speak to Silvia. 'Silvia.'

'Hello, Robbo.'

'Hey, Lexy. Going to school this year?' Lexy shook his head. Robbo glanced at Silvia, surprised.

'He's not been well. I might let him wait till next year.'

'Won't do any harm. See you tomorrow, then.' He gave the little boy a Mintie he pulled from his pocket and went to meet some more arrivals.

Silvia let out a long breath. 'Here we go again, Dad. One more apple harvest.'

But for Silvia, this would be a harvest like no other and several lives, her own included, would be changed forever before it ended.

CHAPTER TWO

Esme Watson had continued to express her thoughts on the 'invasion' all over town and was now doing so to Sister Shirley Dean at the Wandin Valley Clinic. Shirley had of course heard it all before – heavens, she knew it by heart.

'As I was saying in the post office, Shirley, I don't feel safe in my bed with that lot in town. It's not as though my poor little Ralphie could do much to protect me these days.' Since Ralphie was an ancient and arthritic Pekinese, she was probably right on that score.

'I shouldn't worry too much, Esme. I mean, have you ever tried fruit picking? Absolutely exhausting. I'm sure they're all too tired to get up to much rape and pillage.'

Esme wasn't sure if Shirley was having a little dig at her or not. She decided not to pursue it. 'Well I just hope young Dr Bowen will write a prescription for my nerve pills and then I guess I'll somehow manage to get through it.'

'Oh, I'm sure he will, Esme, he's very understanding. He must be off the phone by now, I'll just have a quick word to him before you go in.'

She found Simon not on the phone but gazing out the window. 'Oh, sorry, Shirl. Is there a patient waiting, you should have buzzed me. I was off in a bit of a daydream.'

Shirley looked concerned. Simon wasn't the daydreaming type. 'Is everything alright?'

'Not really, no.'

'Need a motherly shoulder to cry on?'

'Does it come with a strong black coffee?'

'As soon as you've seen Miss Esme Watson.' She passed him Esme's card. Simon tried to suppress a shudder and glanced at the notes. 'Sleeping pills? Diazepam?'

'Try to be kind. It's her armour against the fruit-pickers.'

'What have they ever done to her?'

'To my certain knowledge, not a damn thing. Not in twenty-five years. It's irrational, but there it is. And if I were you, Simon, I'd just play along.'

Simon did not like being told how to practice his very recently acquired skills as a licensed general practitioner. 'That's your medical opinion, Shirley?'

'It is. Unless you want Esme telling the entire district how uncaring and incompetent you are.'

Simon gave a deep, deep sigh. 'Point taken, Sister Dean. I'll endure Miss Watson then.'

Shirley gave him a grin. 'I'll just give you a moment to glance at the Hippocratic Oath, shall I?'

If Simon was feeling somewhat out-of-sorts, the senior partner in the practice was at that moment in the best of spirits. He was at the hospital, his patients there were all doing well, and he was now in the office of his friend and colleague, Marta Kurtesz, the matron. And he could not keep his good news to himself any longer. 'It's a done deal, Marta. I am now a vigneron. Doesn't that sound so much grander than a grape-grower?'

'Oh, Terence, you've done it? You've bought the Eldershaw place? That's wonderful! Congratulations.' She couldn't have been more pleased for him. She wasn't at all sure that a vineyard would fill the gap in Terence's life but if it went even part of the way towards healing old wounds, if it gave him something new to focus on, then it was most definitely, in Marta's view, a good buy.

'Harriet Eldershaw's off to England, she's giving me the keys in two days. I'm sure I'm mad – even Harriet thinks I'm probably mad – there's so much work to be done out there and God knows when I'll find the time to do it but I'm really quite excited.' Nurse Brendan Jones came in and was given the good news. He too was delighted but couldn't resist a dig.

'Wonderful,' he said. 'Someone else Molly can moan to about the weather. The lack of rain or the over-abundance; the frosts, the floods, the pests, the moulds and the mildews … welcome to farming, doctor, what a rich and varied tapestry awaits you.'

'Thank you, Nurse Jones. I'll remember your warm encouragement when I'm asking people to sample my award-winning reds.' The laughter was interrupted by the arrival of a bloodied Bob Hatfield. A known haemophiliac, he was greeted with consternation.

'Oh, Bob! Don't tell me you've been brawling with the pickers already?' said Marta, ushering him towards an exam cubicle.

'Now that's unkind, Matron. As a matter of fact, one of them had a go at my little mate.'

'What, at Cookie?' said Terence, referring to Bob's pal, Vernon Locke.

'Said some things I won't repeat.'

'All the same, Bob. You should know better than to

get involved – Brendan, quick!' Bob, a very large man, chose that moment to pass out. Brendan and Terence between them caught him before he hit the floor and managed to guide his supine body on to the bed.

'Picking season,' Terence said. 'Our favourite time of the year, Marta, isn't it?' Brendan, who had only been in the valley a few months, smiled in all innocence.

'Really?' he said.

Shirley took two cups of coffee into Simon's surgery.

'Thanks, Shirl. Though what I really need after Esme Watson is a double brandy. She makes the apple harvest sound like open warfare.'

'Fortunately, it's nearly all in Esme's far too vivid imagination.'

'Is there any trouble at all?'

'Very seldom. And when there is, Frank Gilroy's there to throw his weight around.'

'I'm sure he'd do an excellent job.' Simon glanced through the open door at the roses on Shirley's desk and wondered why she could never say anything nice about the good sergeant. She saw the glance and ignored it. She knew that half the town saw her tripping down the aisle with Sergeant Gilroy; they had no idea how wrong they were.

'Esme told me you did better than she'd expected.'

'I suppose that's high praise.'

'Oh, indeed. So now you can rest on your laurels, we're done for the day. Barring emergencies.'

'Terence not back from wherever it was?'

'I think he was going to call at the hospital.'

'Oh, right.' Simon paused and couldn't resist. 'Do you *know* where he went? He just muttered about something important.'

'I think he'll want to tell you himself.'

Simon smiled. 'The vineyard, then. Lucky Terence.'

'You want a vineyard?'

'God no! Just a project, a challenge … maybe I should start leaning Sanskrit or something.' Shirley wondered what was really bugging him; whether he was perhaps still upset about his friend in Sydney who had recently scored a job as a registrar at a big teaching hospital. She was even brave enough to mention it but Simon denied any lingering resentment.

'I'm over that, Shirl. Terence made me see that deep down, I have absolutely no desire to be a dermatologist. All those spots and lesions.'

Shirley didn't quite believe him but let it rest. 'What, then? Because you do seem just a tiny bit disgruntled.'

'Restless. That's it. Sounds less peevish, doesn't it? And I'll tell you one thing, I'll be a great deal happier when the damn painters have finished.' Simon had recently rented a pleasant house in Bligh Street but he'd decided, with the landlady's blessing, to get it painted before he moved in. A big mistake, it was taking forever and he was still stuck in his dingy little unit at the motel.

'Have they given you a date?'

'Cunning sods, they say it depends on the weather. How, Shirley? It hasn't rained since Elaine Mackay's funeral.'

'Patience, darling. This is –'

'Please. Don't say this is the country. How could I forget?'

'And that's all that's bugging you? A rather slow paint job?'

'No.' He did not elaborate, he didn't have to. Shirley knew perfectly well that the real source of his malaise was her daughter Vicky. Simon wanted a deep and meaningful relationship with Vicky; she was having none of it.

'Polo,' said Simon suddenly. 'I've been asked to play, what do you think?'

Shirley nearly dropped her coffee. '*Polo*?' And then she remembered Simon had been to visit his cousins, the Smythe-Kings, the nearest thing the district had to landed gentry. 'Oh, of course. The Magnolia Vale connection. Um – can you ride well enough for polo?'

'Yes, Shirl, as a matter of fact I can. And they need an extra player and it might just be a bit of fun. Don't you think?'

'More fun than Sanskrit,' said Shirley.

'I'll see what Vicky thinks, we're having dinner on Wednesday. I can't imagine why she agreed. Sick of my asking her, I suppose.'

'I'm sure she enjoys your intelligent conversation.' Shirley was tempted to add that if Simon really wanted to annoy Vicky, playing polo with the Smythe-King crowd was a great way to go about it. Wisely, she refrained.

Vicky herself was still busy in her veterinary surgery. Her client was Mrs Emily Page, a lady in her early seventies. Vicky liked Emily but then most people did; she was as charming and well-bred as the beautiful Burmese cat she had brought in. Emily suffered from severe rheumatoid arthritis, a condition she tried to ignore with attitude and painkillers though her stoicism was shining a little less brightly these days as the disease tightened its grip.

She was concerned that her beloved cat might have an ear infection but Vicky couldn't find any problem and in fact suspected that something else might have prompted the visit.

'Coco seems absolutely fine, Emily. No signs of infection that I can see. Just keep an eye on it though, in case I've missed something.'

'I'm sure you haven't, Vicky. I'm just worrying about nothing.' Emily sighed. 'Well actually no, I'm not. I've been reading up on Burmese. Coco's only three years old – and they can live to sixteen apparently, something like that. Oh my dear, what on earth was I thinking of?' She sounded quite distraught.

Vicky quickly got a chair and sat her down and Coco immediately leapt onto her lap. Vicky noticed Emily's hands again as she held the cat and tried to stroke it and knew instinctively what the problem was. She spoke very gently. 'Are you worried that one day you may not be able to look after her, Emily?'

Emily nodded. 'I should never have got her. Love at first sight, you see. But really, it was such a selfish thing to do. I knew then this wretched disease would only get worse. Do you think, when the time comes, you'd be able to find a good home for her?'

Vicky almost laughed. 'Oh, Emily. Look at her! She's the most beautiful creature. And so good-natured! Anyone would give her a home, I'd be fighting them off. Please. That's the least of your worries. For now, just enjoy her company. Let tomorrow take care of itself.'

Emily looked a little happier. 'I like that expression. My friend Harriet Eldershaw uses it often. I suppose I'm silly, I can't undo what's done, but at three o'clock in the morning …'

'It's a great time for worrying.'

'It's a very bad habit I've got into, I must try to stop. Thank you, Vicky. I hope I haven't taken up too much of your time. I think I saw Esme Watson arriving just as I came in.'

'Oh dear God. She'll want tranquillizers for Ralphie, the pickers upset him.'

'Perhaps you should check Coco again,' Emily said hastily. 'Just to be on the safe side. Did I mention her back leg? I'm almost sure she was limping last week.'

'I could give Coco a complete physical. Shouldn't take more than an hour.'

'I'm sure it's tempting,' Emily said. 'But we mustn't be cruel.' Vicky sighed and agreed that indeed they shouldn't. Reluctantly she helped Emily out with Coco and ushered Miss Watson and Ralphie in. She was somewhat abashed to find that Ralphie had a nasty cut on his paw. Less so when Esme found a reason to blame the fruit pickers for his misfortune.

As it turned out, Simon did see one more patient that day, a girl of about eight who, like Ralphie, had a nasty cut on her foot. Her mother made a lot less fuss than Esme, however, and Tiffany, the little girl, was a good deal braver than Ralphie. She sucked on the jelly bean Simon gave her while he stitched the wound, and barely winced.

He commended her on her bravery and discovered from her mother that the injury was due to Tiffany's aversion to shoes. The minute she got back from school, off they came. Not such a good idea around the camping ground. Simon realised they were probably pickers.

'Well you'll have to wear shoes for at least two weeks, Tiffany. If that cut got infected, you'd really be in trouble. Do you understand? You have to keep it very clean.'

Tiffany nodded. 'I will.'

They hadn't been gone long when Terence returned.

'Sorry I'm so late back, I hope you weren't run off your feet.'

'No, it wasn't too bad at all.'

'How did you go with Esme Watson, I saw her name in the book.'

'Apparently I passed the test.'

'Oh, well done, that's quite an achievement.'

'And you?' asked Simon. 'Successful afternoon?'

'As I'm sure you'll have guessed, Simon, I was visiting Harriet Eldershaw. And yes, thank you, it was successful, I now own her vineyard. So come upstairs and help me celebrate.'

They shut the clinic and were soon enjoying a very good red in Terence's flat above it. Terence was full of his plans for the place – which he admitted could rapidly send him bankrupt – and Simon was a willing listener, though he did wonder to himself how Terence was going to fit it all in: his work in the practice and at the hospital, the mysterious commitment which took him to Melbourne for at least one weekend every month – and now the vineyard.

'Are you going to change the name?' Simon asked.

'I'm not sure. I mean if I did – what would I call the place? And Eldershaw Estate has a nice ring to it, don't you think?'

'It does sounds serious,' Simon agreed. 'Like "we've been doing wine here for generations".'

They bandied around a few alternatives but came up with nothing better before they finally returned to things medical. Terence thought they'd be in for a busy couple of weeks with the pickers; he mentioned that Bob Hatfield had already been in a fight. Simon admitted that he'd been a coward where Esme was concerned; he'd caved in and prescribed her usual pills. And he mentioned the little girl who'd been so brave.

'They were nice people, Terence. I kept thinking – what is Esme on about?'

'I can rarely see what Esme Watson is on about. But the little girl – did you check that her tetanus shots were up to date?'

Simon looked surprised. 'No, I didn't. She was eight – she's not due for a booster yet.'

'That's assuming she was fully vaccinated in the first place. These people lead pretty tough lives, Simon. On the road the whole time, their health care's a bit haphazard. Things like immunization can easily get forgotten.'

Simon was mortified. 'I should have thought.'

'You will next time. What was their name?'

'Brownlow. The little girl's Tiffany.'

'We'll hunt them down in the morning. It's probably fine.' He refilled their glasses. 'In a couple of years we should be awash with this stuff. Isn't that a beautiful thought?'

Simon could only agree.

CHAPTER THREE

While the doctors were lost in a romantic idyll involving cool cellars lined with large oak barrels full of maturing wine – quite forgetting for a moment the work involved to achieve this – they themselves were under discussion at Harriet Eldershaw's dining-table.

'I was so relieved when Terence decided to buy the place,' said Harriet. 'I didn't want to sell to just anyone. But he seems such a nice man.'

'He is,' said Emily Page. 'He'll get the vineyard on its feet again. And look after your memories.'

'That's it,' said Harriet. 'I'm afraid I'll come back one day and not recognise the place.'

Emily smiled. 'Terence Elliott isn't the sort to turn it into a holiday resort.'

'You know him well, don't you?'

'Very well. He's a good friend as well as being my doctor. Though young Simon sent my last lot of scripts out so maybe I'll see him next time.'

It was Harriet's turn to smile. 'And is young Simon aware of your connection with his family?'

'He is not. I intend to surprise him.' Emily Page allowed herself something like a giggle. Harriet poured them both another glass of champagne. It was, after all, a special occasion. They clinked glasses. Harriet noticed how Emily held on to hers with both hands to prevent it slipping but did not comment. She knew that Emily hated to talk about her illness.

'Have a wonderful trip, Harriet.'

'I wish you were coming with me.'

But they both knew that was out of the question. 'You will write? I can't imagine how much London must have changed, I haven't been there for twenty years. Tell me about the little things you don't see on television.'

'Of course I'll write.'

'I'll miss you so much, Harriet.'

'I won't be gone forever.'

'It might still be too long.'

'Don't say that, Emily. Promise you'll wait till I get back. Promise me.'

Emily reached across the table and took her friend's hand.

'I can't make promises I might not keep. You know that.'

When Vicky finally got home from the surgery, fixating on a hot shower and bowl of pasta, she was less than thrilled to find that Shirley already had dinner under way. Shirley Dean had never been much of a cook but she chose to ignore this fact and Vicky had been suffering as a result for close on twenty-six years. It was more than enough but since Shirley was one of those people who saw food as fuel rather than as a sensual pleasure, it was hard to bring about any changes.

'Hello darling,' she said brightly as Vicky came in. 'You're awfully late, dinner's almost ready.' Shirley herself was sitting under her pyramid, finishing a meditation session. She felt the pyramid improved her aura and helped to get rid of stagnant energy.

'I was busy, Mum, animals are so inconsiderate about when they get sick. What are we having?'

'Oh, a sort of curry thingummy. Rice is nearly cooked.'

Vicky didn't like the sound of it at all. She went to the stove and lifted a lid.

'You did put water in with the rice?'

'Chicken stock. I'm using the absorption method.'

'I'd say it all got absorbed long ago.'

'It couldn't have!'

'It did.' Vicky turned the stove off. She upended the saucepan over a plate. No rice issued forth. Shirley came to look at the solid mass.

'I can't understand it,' Shirley said.

'How long were you under the pyramid, Mum?'

'Not long.' Shirley sounded vague. Vicky rolled her eyes.

'Just as well you're not trying to win Frank Gilroy with your culinary skills, you'd have no hope.'

'When will you and everyone else understand that I have no interest in the man?'

'When you stop protesting too much.' Vicky scraped the rice into the garbage bin and went to answer the phone. 'I bet that's him now.'

'Don't answer it. He always rings when we're about to eat.'

'But we're not about to eat, are we?' She picked up the phone.

'I'm not here!' Shirley hissed. 'I have disappeared, I've bought a one-way ticket to outer Mongolia!'

'Hello, Sergeant Gilroy, how nice to hear from you,' Vicky said into the phone. 'Yes, lovely weather … Mum? No, I'm sorry, she's not here at the moment.' But Shirley had had a sudden change of heart and was tugging at Vicky's arm and making signs she wanted the phone. 'Oh, hang on, I just heard the door slam … yes, here she is.'

Vicky handed over the phone, looking somewhat bewildered – but only for a moment.

'Frank? Shirley. Just got in … Yes, busy day … Look, I was wondering if you'd like to come to dinner? Say Wednesday? I've got a couple of new recipes I'm dying to try out … you can? Lovely, see you then.'

Shirley hung up and turned to look at Vicky's appalled face.

'You can't.'

'Of course I can. I'm not that bad a cook.'

'You are. You're worse.'

'Nonsense. I'm sure Frank will enjoy anything I put in front of him.'

'I'll get in plenty of ipecac. I'll put the hospital on standby. You're an evil woman.'

'Oh darling, it's for his own good. Somehow I've got to make him understand that we just aren't suited. I mean, me married to a policeman? It's just ridiculous. Isn't it?'

'If you say so, Mum. Now what do you want for dinner?'

'There's still the curry.'

Vicky had sneaked a look at the 'curry'. 'Let's save that, shall we? I'll whip up some pasta.'

Shirley smiled wickedly. 'Curries improve after a day or two. I could give it to Frank. Go all Indian.'

'Only if you want to kill him.'

Shirley ignored this remark and poured them both a glass of wine while Vicky got on with the pasta. 'You know who Frank needs? Someone like Pat Turner.'

'*Pat Turner*?' Vicky was not impressed.

'What's wrong with Pat? She's good-natured, she can cook.'

'She's been looking after her tyrant of a father far too long. She's had all the life squashed out of her.'

'You make her sound like a dead beetle.'

'Artie treats her like some lower form of existence. No, she's not right for Frank Gilroy.'

'Well I disagree. I think they'd be very good together.' Shirley added the clincher. 'Pat's a very keen gardener.'

'Stop it, Mum.'

'Stop what?'

'Match-making.'

'Don't be silly, darling. It's self-defence.'

Match-making was high on the agenda at the Jones farm that evening; indeed, it was being discussed in some detail over a chicken casserole.

'I rang Gary Percival,' Molly was saying, 'and he's happy to mate his boar with Doris. I told him it'll probably be sometime this week.'

'Do you have to get Doris over to them?'

'Good heavens no, the gentleman calls on the lady. Landrace Huntington III will visit her here.'

'Well that's a blessing,' Brendan said. 'I doubt if she'd fit in the station-wagon.'

'I just hope she likes him,' Molly said. 'You never know with arranged marriages.'

'I'm sure it'll be love at first sight. Just like us.'

'I hope so. I want Doris to have lots of babies.'

Brendan shook his head. 'So you can get soppy over every single one of them.'

'Don't be silly, Brendan. So we can sell them and make some money at last. Real money. It's time this farm started paying its way. I don't want you to feel the burden of being the sole breadwinner.'

'Molly. It's not a burden. We've only been here a few months, you've got to give it time.' And he put his arms around her and held her tightly and kissed her.

'Brendan?'

'Mm?'

'It's not fair.'

He knew what she was going to say: why should the damn pig get to have babies while she had to wait? 'Darling … one more year. We both agreed. Time to settle in here.'

Molly went back to her casserole. Not happy. 'Maybe I should do some fruit-picking. Earn some extra money.'

'Maybe we should finish dinner and have an early night.'

She gave him a look. 'Only if you help with the washing up.'

'Couldn't we leave it till morning?'

'Rats, Brendan. Cockroaches.'

'It's nice to share.'

She caved. 'Just this once, then.'

The Wandin Valley Camping Ground was run by the local council and sprawled over several acres between the football ground and the river. Like the waterhole further upstream, it was shaded by she-oaks and willows and was quite a pleasant spot. Not long after he moved to the Valley, Terence Elliot had made it his business to approach the council and try to get better conditions for the fruit pickers. As a result, most of them took advantage of the special rates offered at the ground and the fact that the school bus stopped at the entrance in the morning to collect their kids. Small things but they helped.

Tonight the ground was almost full but it was also quiet, even though it wasn't yet nine o'clock. A few grey nomads sat sharing yarns and beers down by the water but the pickers were mostly getting ready for bed. As Shirley Dean had said to Esme Watson, picking is hard work. It's perhaps not so bad if you work for an hourly rate but when the orchardist pays by the box and especially when – like Bruce Cameron – he imposes a quota, then the pressure is relentless. It's survival of the fittest, or rather the quickest and if you don't keep up you soon get your marching orders. For older people like Alex Popovich it was nothing short of brutal.

Alex was thinking about it now in the tiny cabin he shared with Silvia and Lexy, gearing himself up for the long day ahead, telling himself he could do it. He was making hot chocolate, an extravagance but they'd only had rice and some vegetables for tea. He was listening to Lexy, who was sitting on the steps, chatting to the little girl from next door.

'I'm going to school tomorrow,' Tiffany said. 'Are you coming?'

'Nah.'

'Why not?'

'Mum says I'm too sick to go.'

'I've got a big cut on my foot, the doctor had to stitch it up. I'm still going. I reckon you ought to come, Lexy, they're okay at the school here. Ask your mum again. Night.'

'Night, Tiffany.'

Silvia was returning from the shower block. She saw Tiffany limp into her cabin and returned her wave and then was almost knocked off her feet by a young man walking with his head down and his eyes half-closed and his arms hugging his chest.

'Watch where you're going!' he said.

Silvia couldn't believe it. 'What? You walked straight into me!'

He stared at her with glazed eyes. 'Did I?'

'Yes! What's the matter with you? You're shaking, are you sick or something?'

'Don't feel too good, to be honest. Sorry.'

He veered off the track towards a small tent. Silvia watched him for a moment then shrugged it off and went back to the cabin. She was grateful for the chocolate and managed to smile at Alex.

'I need this. Some idiot nearly knocked me over.'

'Drunk?'

'I don't think so. He looked sick, to be honest. It's alright. Lexy, you should be in bed.' She ruffled his hair.

'I was talking to Tiffany.'

'I saw.'

Alex took the opportunity presented. 'She was telling Lexy how he should go to school.'

'We've talked about it, Dad. He's not ready.' Her tone was flat, she was not prepared to discuss it. Alex, who felt that she was over-protective, that she'd wrap the boy in cotton wool and smother him, saw the relief on Lexy's face and didn't push it. But they both knew he disagreed with the decision.

'I think I will take a little walk before bed,' he said. 'It helps me to sleep.' He went out into the cool night air and walked the length of the camping ground; past the cabin where Tiffany's mum was getting her things ready for school and past the tent where the strange young man was trying to sleep. Their paths would cross before too long. He walked as far as the football ground and there he lay on the grass and looked at the sky and picked out the constellations and realised that these southern stars were now as familiar as those he'd known when he was young. It was time he started teaching his grandson about the stars. About so many things. He did not want him to grow up thinking there was nothing but work and worry in the world. God knew there was plenty of that but there was also an infinite universe full of mystery and wonder out there. In his darkest moments Alex liked to contemplate its enormity, it always helped to put his problems into perspective.

CHAPTER FOUR

The next morning, the first real day of the Wandin Valley apple harvest, Terence arrived quite early at Bruce Cameron's orchard. The pickers were already hard at work when he parked the Nissan by the gate; he waved to one he knew by sight from seasons past and went inside. He was there to see Bruce's wife, Edie, who had a number of ailments, some serious, some less so. She was asthmatic and seemed unable to manage her condition very well and she had constant abdominal cramps which she was certain heralded the onset of cancer. Since tests had shown nothing, Terence thought they were more likely due to irritable bowel syndrome, itself exacerbated by her third problem, namely her husband. Terence did not like Bruce, whom he'd long ago pegged as a bully.

He spent some time with Edie. He suggested that some mild exercise, especially swimming, would be good for her asthma and prescribed an antidepressant which he felt might improve both her spirits and her irritable bowel. He was quite sure she *was* depressed and wasn't surprised in the least.

He did his best to hide his antipathy when he talked to Bruce after the consultation.

'So what's the verdict, doc? Thought she looked okay myself but she always finds something to whinge about, old Edie does.'

Terence could barely contain his anger. 'Your wife's got very painful cramps and she's asthmatic, Bruce. Meaning it's very often hard for her to breathe. That's enough for anyone to whinge about. I do think some swimming would help her asthma though.'

'Swimming? What, in the river?'

'There's a very nice pool in Burrigan. You could take her over, have some lunch afterwards, that'd do her the world of good. A bit of TLC is what Edie needs.'

'That's all very well, doc, but it's harvest time in case you hadn't noticed. I can't go charging off to Burrigan at the drop of a hat. It's not as though Edie's really crook, is she?'

'Not yet, she isn't. And the idea is to stop that happening. I've left some prescriptions. You should get them filled as soon as possible.'

'Right you are.'

'Encourage her not to stay in bed. Gentle activity, that's the go. And I don't mean stripping apple trees.'

'Pity. I could do with the extra help.'

Terence was not amused. 'Before I go – got anyone picking by the name of Brownlow?'

'A young couple. Why?'

'I just need a quick word with them, if that's alright, it's about their little girl.'

Bruce nodded. 'Second row, down at the end. The blonde.'

'Thanks. And don't forget – TLC.'

Terence left Cameron to harass the pickers. He had no trouble finding Janice Brownlow and was delighted to learn that Tiffany had received all recommended childhood vaccinations.

'Dr Bowen felt he should have asked you, and as I was coming over here anyway … I hope you don't mind us checking.'

'Of course not, nice of you to bother. No, last year we were picking up in northern New South Wales and you know half the kids got measles? I made sure then that Tiffany was up to date.'

'Good for you. How's her foot?'

'It can't be too bad, she would go to school this morning. I sent a note for the teacher though.'

'Dr Bowen does very good needlework.' Janice laughed at that and went back to her work and Terence headed back to his car. On the way, he heard a voice call.

'Lexy! Lexy!' Silvia Popovich was looking for her son. Cameron appeared from between the trees.

'The kid's around here somewhere. Saw him not long ago. Best you get back to work.'

'I just like to know where he is, Mr Cameron.'

'And I like to know my apples are being picked.'

'They will be. Honestly.' Relief spread over her face as Lexy came running towards her. 'Oh, there he is.'

'Told you.'

Cameron shook his head and left them but Terence was staring at the child who was very thin but had a strange little pot belly. Cameron walked past him on his way to the house.

'You see what I'm up against, doc? I'm running a kindergarten here.' As Alex joined Silvia he added, 'Not to mention an old people's home.'

Terence decided to ignore this. 'That little boy – Lexy?'

'Yeah. What about him?'

'He looks like he's got malnutrition.'

'Come off it, doc! He's surrounded by apple trees! I do let them eat the odd bit of fruit, I'm not that much of a Scrooge.'

'But he's so thin. And that pot belly …' Terence was still concerned.

'Well I pay enough for them to feed their kids. None of our business, I reckon.'

Terence, who knew exactly what they got paid, refrained from comment. He glanced at his watch. 'I must dash, I've got another call before surgery, don't forget those prescriptions for Edie, will you?'

'No worries. Get 'em done today.'

Terence wished he could believe him.

Emily Page had endured a very bad night and morning had brought no relief from the never-ending pain. She was therefore in no mood at all to tolerate the shenanigans going on next door. Nor, for the life of her, could Emily imagine how Pat Turner put up with it. Pat lived with her father, Artie. She'd been his carer for sixteen long years since her mother died. She was patient, loyal and loving to the point of saintliness. Artie was a selfish, cantankerous, foul-mouthed curmudgeon. The more Pat gave, the more Artie demanded. It was reaching the point where something would very shortly snap.

Artie was confined to a wheelchair due to a workplace accident a few years before he was due to retire. However, sympathy for his plight had long since dried up in Wandin Valley. As Esme Watson was wont to say, we all have our cross to bear and Artie Turner's was far from being the heaviest she'd seen, and for once Esme got no argument.

Once a month, a community bus took elderly residents, including some from the nursing home, on a day-long outing. They would visit places of local interest and have lunch and a flutter on the pokies at the RSL club. It was a nice change for the oldies and it gave their carers a day's respite. Artie normally went without too much fuss; he quite enjoyed lording it over the people from the nursing home, whom he somehow regarded as an inferior species, even those he'd known since boyhood, even those who were more able-bodied than he. He liked to think of them as enfeebled, incarcerated in something akin to a prison. He was quite sure he would never join them. He had Pat.

On this particular morning, however, Artie decided the bus was not for him.

This was unfortunate since Pat had a toothache and badly needed to see her dentist. She explained the situation gently but firmly. Artie needed to get on the bus; he'd enjoy the day once they got going. Could he please just help her out and co-operate? Artie was having none of it.

'I don't know how you can ask me, after the night I've had. Not a wink of sleep, I was in such pain.'

'Dad, that's rubbish, you snored your head off.'

'You were dreaming, girl. Agony, that's what I had to put up with. All night! And now you expect me to sit on a bus with a bunch of morons, all they ever talk about is their aches and pains, all the pills they take, none of them know what suffering is! I'm not going, I tell you! I bloody well don't feel up to it!'

Pat tried to remonstrate. They were on the front porch and as the tirade increased in volume and the language became less and less delicate, she cringed at what the neighbours must be thinking. Then Emily Page came up the path to let Artie know.

'They're just about ga-ga, most of them, lost their marbles, you want me to spend a whole day with them?'

'Oh do be quiet, Artie, we've all heard more than enough.'

'Come to give us your two bob's worth have you, Emily?'

'And put that wretched cigarette out,' said Pat.

The bus pulled up outside. So did Terence Elliott, who paused for a brief word with the driver before hurrying in to join them.

'Let me tell you, Artie,' said Emily. 'You're the one who's starting to sound as though you're a sandwich short of a picnic. I have never heard such rubbish! Or such language. Ah, Terence.' Artie quickly stubbed his cigarette out.

'Emily. Pat, I'm sorry I'm late. Artie, you're not causing any trouble, are you?'

'I'm not going, doc. Don't feel up to it.'

'That's a pity. The driver tells me they're having lunch at that nice pub out at Widgeera. Very good tucker.'

'Got no appetite.'

'Best roast pork I've ever had. And you know they brew their own beer? Excellent it is too. Never mind, I'm sure Pat can leave you a sandwich.'

'She can't leave me here alone!'

'She hasn't any choice, she needs to see the dentist. What's it to be?'

Artie gave a mighty sigh of resignation and nodded at the bus. Terence smiled.

'Sensible man. I hope I didn't see you smoking before, did I?' He wheeled him away.

'Thank God for Dr Elliott,' Pat said.

'Honestly, Pat, I don't know how you put up with Arthur.'

'He's my dad. What else can I do?'

Emily thought to herself that patricide might be a sensible option. Pat took herself off to the dentist and Emily went back to the peace of her own garden and stood for a while, leaning on her stick which she hated but needed, enjoying the morning sun. There was still some warmth in it, thank goodness; she wished that winter would have a fit of the sulks and refuse to come this year.

She closed her eyes and remembered a time when she loved winter; long walks on crisp mornings and holidays in the snow. Hard to believe what a good skier she'd been. She opened her eyes at the sound of a car. Someone had just pulled up at her gate in a most delightfully flashy sportscar. She did not know the vehicle but she would have recognised the driver anywhere, even though they had never been introduced: that mop of blond hair falling over his face, so he had to keep tossing it back, the confident stride as he came up her path, carrying a large box he'd retrieved from the passenger seat; his every gesture took her back almost half a century. As for the smile, that too was painfully familiar, though she managed to adopt a look of polite enquiry as he approached.

'Mrs Page? We haven't actually met, not in person that is, but I'm Simon Bowen.'

'Dr Bowen. At last. How very nice.' She held out her hand, then laughed, realising the parcel precluded handshakes. 'I'm sorry, could you perhaps bring it in? Is that from the post office?'

'Yes, I was there when it arrived and Ida Dugdale was looking for someone to drop it off so I volunteered.' He followed Emily inside.

'How very kind.'

'Not at all, it's on my way to the clinic.'

'No really, I'm most appreciative. It's my books, you see, and I'm right out of reading material.'

'You don't use the library?'

'Oh, I do, yes, but they can't keep up with me. These come from a publisher friend of mine, advance copies. He knows I'm a truly voracious reader – well, not much else to do, these days – and he keeps me supplied.'

'Well good for him. Do you need help opening the box?'

That was an offer Emily accepted. 'Do you read yourself?'

'More than I used to. Country evenings, you know – it's a good book or the telly. Or medical journals.' He enquired about her health while he cut through string and sticky tape. 'And how are you, Mrs. Page?'

'I think the phrase is, as well as can be expected, doctor.'

'Simon, please.'

'Simon, then. And you must call me Emily.'

'Well if you need a home visit, just let us know.'

'I can still drive a little. Most days. Well. Some days.'

'We're here to help, Emily. You have only to ask.'

'Thank you. I'll remember. And thank you so much for the books.'

'My great pleasure. I'm delighted we've finally met.' Simon felt like kissing her hand, she had that effect on him, gracious, that was the word. But he shook it instead and let himself out and left Emily thinking it was as if Charlie had, briefly, come back to her. She laughed at the fancy and turned her attention to the books.

Molly Jones had spent the morning, or part of it, explaining to Doris the joyous event which would soon take place. It's doubtful if Doris got the message since Molly, swept up in the romance of it all, chose to couch it in rather Austenesque terms. Landrace Huntington III would call on Doris one day soon and present his credentials. It would be nice, Molly said, if she were to look upon his suit favourably. Doris gave a grunt which might have been acquiescence and went to sleep. Molly was disappointed. She felt a little frisson of excitement would not have been unseemly. Molly was so busy with her play-acting that she did not notice the small boy lurking on the other side of the wood-heap, listening in wide-eyed amazement to every word.

Back inside, Molly busied herself with her sewing. She was finishing off a dress she was making for Vicky Dean, payment for veterinary services rendered. Molly had been careful to tone down her own highly original style for the more conservative Vicky but now wondered if she hadn't gone too far, if the dress wasn't a little bit boring. She knew it was beautifully cut, she hadn't spent years in the fashion industry for nothing, but the colour worried her, that silvery blue. Molly herself loved everything bright, red, green, orange, purple; when Brendan wanted to tease her he called her his zinnia girl.

She hung the dress up and looked at it from all angles and decided that, after all, it would probably suit Vicky. She hoped so. She enjoyed sewing, she thought she could possibly make it a profitable little sideline. Something to see them through the 115 days before Doris could be expected to give birth. Supposing, of course, that all went well tomorrow.

Feeling peckish, Molly started to make herself a salad roll. The radio was on and she hummed along to Lionel Ritchie and Diana Ross singing 'Endless Love'. She hoped Doris would feel endless love for Landrace Huntington III. The roll grew bigger. Cheese, lettuce, tomato, ham, cucumber, sprouts, a dash of mayo. She was salivating. The song faded away and it was then that Molly suddenly got the feeling that she wasn't alone. She turned around to the open back door. A little boy was standing there, staring at her. Molly, relieved to find it wasn't an axe murderer, smiled.

'Hello. What's your name?'

He said nothing.

'Well I'm Molly. I haven't seen you before, did you come with the fruit pickers?'

A faint nod. Molly saw how thin he was. 'You look like maybe you missed your breakfast. How about a salad roll? I just made it.' She picked it up and held it out towards him. 'Salad and ham and cheese, you're very welcome.'

The boy grabbed the roll out of her hand. 'Ta.' He fled.

Molly called after him, 'Come back any time!' She wondered why he looked so undernourished and why he wasn't in school. It was none of her business, Molly knew that. But if he did come back, she'd do her best to find out.

CHAPTER FIVE

Silvia was unaware that her son was arousing so much interest. She was concerned that he had once again vanished from her sight but did not dare stop to go looking for him. Alex gently told her to stop worrying, the boy would be around somewhere, she had to let him spread his wings and learn to fly. He stopped himself from saying that if he were at school she would not have to fret about him every minute of the day, she could get on with her work knowing that he was safe. It was then that Bill Ferguson turned up.

'G'day,' he said. 'Just wanted to let you know I found that tyre, I've left it by your wagon.'

'This is very kind,' said Alex. 'You must tell us what we owe you.'

'No, honest, like I said, nothing. It was just cluttering up the shed.'

'What can I say, then? Thank you.'

'Yes, it is very generous,' Silvia added.

'My pleasure. Oh – here's your boy.'

Lexy arrived with the remains of Molly's roll.

Silvia's relief spilled over into anger. 'Lexy, where have you been? Where did you get that?'

'Lady gave it to me.'

'What lady? You can't go taking food from strangers!'

'She was nice. She had green legs and pink ribbons!'

'Lexy, don't tell stories!'

Bill was grinning. 'It's okay. I think he's met Molly Jones. Owns the farm next door. And she *is* nice. Bit of a weirdo though.'

'Molly, yeah. She's weird alright.'

'You shouldn't go bothering people, Lexy.'

Bill wondered why Silvia was so anxious about everything. 'Molly wouldn't be bothered. Not by a kid. She's a lot of fun. Just wears these really way out clothes.'

'Oh. Sort of hippy, is she?' Silvia actually smiled and Bill thought how nice it made her look. His ex-wife, Kerry-Anne, had forgotten how to smile by the time she walked out on him.

The weird Molly Jones was by then in Vicky Dean's surgery. She had The Dress with her but was nervous about showing it to Vicky and was prattling on instead about Doris's big day which was fast approaching. Vicky was reassuring. It wasn't as if Doris had never done this before; she was in fact an old hand. She would probably relish the idea of motherhood once more.

'And now,' said Vicky, 'if you've got some sort of livestock in that bag, perhaps we should get it out?'

'Oh! No. No, it's a dress. That is, your dress. If you like it.'

'It's finished already? Show me!'

Molly took the dress out and displayed it on its hanger. Vicky was, quite clearly, thrilled. 'Oh, Molly, I love it. You're a miracle-worker. And your timing's spot on, now I've got something to wear tomorrow night!' She held the dress against herself. 'What do you think?'

'I think it'll really suit you. What's on tomorrow?'

'Dinner with Simon Bowen.' She pulled a face.

'I thought you'd said no?'

'I have. Over and over. So I thought I'd say yes instead and let him see how totally unsuited we are.' Vicky grinned, unaware how much like her mother she sounded.

'Poor Simon. You're going to look ravishing.'

'You really think?' Molly nodded. 'Great. Do him good to realise he can't have everything.' Molly wondered, not for the first time, if Vicky's feelings for Simon were not just a little mixed up.

'So you're happy to take the dress in payment for our vet bill?'

'Oh Molly, of course I am! I'm getting an absolute bargain. We can make it a regular thing if you like.'

'That'd be terrific.'

As Vicky was showing Molly out, they found Liz Anderson waiting. She was there about a talk Vicky was going to give the junior classes and the three women got chatting. To Molly's delight, Liz too admired the dress and asked if she would consider making something for her. Molly went off feeling that if she and Doris both did their bit, then catastrophe could be yet be avoided. Meaning that she would not need to ask her mother Caroline for a loan.

Molly called at the hospital on the way home to see Brendan. He was busy with a patient and she had a few words with Marta Kurtesz while she waited. Molly had had her reservations about Marta at first; not only was she Brendan's boss, she possessed a cool European sophistication that Molly knew she herself could never hope to achieve; it was handed out at birth. Marta, however, was so grateful to have someone of Brendan's experience on her staff and sang his praises so frequently that Molly was soon won over.

'So how is farming life treating you?' Marta was asking.

'Oh, it's up and down. The Department of Agriculture confirmed what Vicky Dean said – the soil's terrible, so I've got to work on that. But there's one spot where I *might* be able to grow some vegetables, so perhaps we won't starve.'

Marta grinned. 'I'm sure you will make a go of it, Molly. Oh, here's Brendan now, I'll let him give you the bad news.' She left them.

'You're not going to be late?'

'Sorry, darling. Ruth Hammond's kid was sent home from school sick. I'll be through about nine, can you cope without me?'

'I'll try. I had a strange little kid visit me today – one of the pickers. He took a salad roll and disappeared. Maybe he'll come again and keep me company. Otherwise, there's always the rats.'

'I can't understand why the poison didn't work.'

'They thought it was a treat.'

'Well ring if you have any problems.'

'Brendan. I'll be fine.' Which did not mean the night would be without incident.

Emily Page was sitting in her garden reading. She was already well into Albert Facey's 'A Fortunate Life' which would not come out till later in the year. Emily was enjoying Mr Facey's memoir very much, as millions of others would eventually do also. She thought that she too had had a fortunate life, her wretched disease notwithstanding. She'd had a happy childhood, a good education, she'd travelled, loved, married, raised three pleasant children. Compared to poor Pat Turner, she'd been singularly blessed. She had noticed Pat come to the front door once or twice, checking for the community bus and had waved and smiled. She hoped the bus had somehow managed to leave Artie behind in Widgeera or Magnolia Vale or anywhere. An unchristian thought but Emily had long ago abandoned many of the Anglican tenets under which she had been raised. She thought Artie, whom she'd known since childhood, deserved whatever he got.

Pat Turner wasn't quite brave enough to allow herself such iconoclastic notions. She would have expected the hand of God to smite her down. Pat had an abscessed tooth. The dentist had drained it and given her antibiotics and painkillers and while she was feeling slightly better she was anything but thrilled when the bus did at last pull up outside her gate.

She put on a brave face and hurried out to help the driver with Artie's chair. She could hear Artie the moment the door opened. He was singing at the top of his voice an old Max Miller song, the one about girls who say one thing but hopefully mean another. Pat was nearly dying of embarrassment. 'Is that the worst you've had to put up with?' she asked the driver?

'Afraid not, Pat. We had 'The Mayor of Bayswater' a while back, that raised a few eyebrows.'

'I'm sorry, Fred. There's no stopping him.'

'Never mind, love. Just Artie's way of dealing with things.'

They got the wheelchair to the door and the ever-patient Fred helped Artie into it. He did not receive any thanks.

'Off you go then,' Artie said. 'Back to God's waiting room.'

'We'll see you next month,' said Fred.

'I'll still be here,' said Artie. 'But that lot? I wouldn't be putting any money on it.' He was already lighting a cigarette.

'Do stop it, Dad. That's a terrible thing to say.'

'Your father says terrible things all the time.' It was one of the old ladies, who could not keep quiet any longer.

'I'm sorry,' said Pat again. 'I'm sure he didn't mean to upset you.'

'Yes I did,' said Artie. 'I had a damn awful time and I don't care who I upset. Don't know what Doc Elliott was on about either, bloody dreadful pub. I hope you've got something decent for my tea, Pat, I'm starving, I couldn't eat a skerrick at lunchtime.' He tried to wheel himself away.

'Aren't you going to say thank you?'

'What the hell for?' Artie turned his back on the bus and its occupants once and for all.

'Don't worry, Pat,' Fred said. 'He'll get over it. And he did eat quite a good lunch.' He got back into the driver's seat and waved goodbye, as did one or two of the others, leaving Pat almost in tears.

'How can you do that, Dad? Those are nice people, how can you be so rude?'

Emily, who had heard every word, called out to her over the fence, all sweetness and light.

'Pat dear, why don't you get Artie settled and pop over for a restorative sherry?'

'She can't leave me alone!'

'You might have to get used to being alone, Arthur. Since you're hell-bent on making yourself unfit for human company. Do come if you feel like it, Pat.'

'Thank you,' said Pat. 'I just might.'

But Emily knew she wouldn't. She didn't have the heart for the battle that would ensue if she tried. Emily didn't have much strength left for battles herself but the liberation of Pat Turner was one she intended to win while she still had time.

***

Vicky Dean was out at Cameron's orchard, visiting another of Wandin Valley's less congenial male citizens. She did not much care for Bruce Cameron, she was not comfortable with any man who treated his dogs better than his wife. She also resented the fact that Cameron expected her to make a house call for a puppy but would baulk when she charged him extra. She was trying to examine the little dog on a table in the packing shed, hardly ideal conditions.

'It would have been better if you'd brought him into the surgery, Mr. Cameron.'

'I can't leave the place while the pickers are here! Never know what they'll get up to.'

Vicky smiled. 'What, afraid they'll steal the crop and disappear, never to be seen again?'

'Riff-raff,' said Cameron. 'I'll bet Sandy's caught something from one of their mangy dogs.'

'What Sandy's caught between his toes is a grass seed,' said Vicky, trying not to sound smug. 'It's caused an abscess. And I'm afraid I can't treat it here, he'll need an anaesthetic.'

'Won't it just work its way out?'

'It could work its way right up his leg, Mr Cameron, and cause a lot more damage. You need to bring him in right away.'

To Vicky's satisfaction, she made Cameron plead. 'It's not just the pickers, Vicky. It's my wife, Edie. She's sick in bed … are you sure you couldn't do it here? It's her pup, see.'

That clinched it, of course. Vicky performed the procedure on a table in the Camerons' laundry. Half-way through, she noticed a small boy watching fascinated from the doorway and was appalled when Cameron yelled at him to get out.

'Go on, go! You got no business past the orchard!'

Terrified, the child fled but not before Vicky noticed

his little pot belly.

'He wasn't doing any harm,' she said mildly.

'Like I said. Riff-raff. Next thing, he'll be in the house, nicking stuff.'

Vicky wondered why he didn't pick his damn apples himself. She was very glad when the small operation was successfully completed and had no compunction in charging Cameron a great deal more than her normal rate.

Shirley Dean and the doctors were having an after work drink in Terence's flat. Terence was telling them about Artie's little performance that morning.

'I do think,' Shirley said, 'that if Pat took to him with a meat cleaver she'd get off. Justifiable homicide.'

'Risky,' said Terence.

'Not if it was an all-female jury.'

'Is he really that bad?' asked Simon. 'I don't recall meeting Artie.'

'You'd remember if you had,' said Shirley. 'Neanderthal man.'

'And Bruce Cameron's another,' said Terence. 'He seems to think Edie's malingering. I wish he'd get sick for a week or two, just so he knows how it feels to be dependent on others.'

'Fit as a mallee bull,' said Shirley. 'Always was.'

'I saw a little boy out at Cameron's – son of one of the pickers – who's really got me puzzled. I don't think he's fit at all.'

'What's the problem?'

'Painfully thin with a little pot belly. Looks for all the world like he's suffering from malnutrition.'

'That's hardly likely, is it?'

'All those apples to eat?' Shirley smiled.

'I'm saying that's what it looked like. Of course it's not *likely* … but it happens.'

'Well if he were malnourished, he'd be pretty lethargic, wouldn't he?' said Simon. 'I mean, did he seem to have much energy?'

'That's a good point. I didn't see him for long but come to think of it, he was running around.'

'So … pot belly. What else is there?'

'Umbilical hernia, maybe. Hard to say without checking him out.'

'So why not go to the camping ground and do it?' said the ever-practical Shirley.

Terence and Simon exchanged a look. 'She would,' said Simon. 'She'd just rock up and demand to see the kid.'

'Made of sterner stuff than me, I'm afraid,' said Terence.

'No doubt about that,' said Shirley tartly. 'For heaven's sake, you're always banging on about how hard it is for the fruit pickers to get adequate health care. Well here's a small kid with a possible serious illness and you have a chance to be pro-active. But of course I'm not a doctor.'

She got up. 'Thanks for the drink. I have to go home and hunt up some recipes, I'm having Sergeant Gilroy to dinner tomorrow.' She swept out. She was just a little cross.

The doctors sipped their drinks. 'She's right of course,' said Terence eventually.

'She often is.'

'Maybe I can find an excuse to go out to the orchard again.'

'Good idea.'

'Did you know about the dinner?' Simon shook his head. 'Poor Frank. She's up to no good. She's the most terrible cook.'

Simon sighed. 'Maybe that's why Vicky agreed to come out with me. To avoid it.'

'I'm sure it's not,' said Terence but he didn't sound sure at all.

'I think I might have a little more wine after all,' said Simon.

After she left the hospital, Molly had braved the supermarket, resenting almost everything she bought there. There were three large bags of the stuff, half a trolley full, and Molly felt that for a couple who wanted to be self-sufficient they had a very long way to go, even while accepting that she was never likely to produce her own coffee, tea and toilet paper in Wandin Valley.

She got home and parked the car close to the back gate. She yelled to Doris that she'd be out to feed her soon and lugged the shopping inside. She noticed that the back door was open but wasn't really fussed. She knew she was sloppy about locking up, this was the country after all, that was one of the nice things about living here. She dropped the bags on the kitchen table with a thud; they'd been heavy and she was glad to put them down.

'Now for the worst bit. Putting it all aw-' She thought she heard a noise and broke off to listen. 'Anyone there?' Then she smiled. 'I know! It's you, isn't it, kid? Are you hungry again? Don't be afraid, it's okay!'

But it wasn't Lexy and it wasn't okay. A man rushed out from the bedroom and shoved her out of the way with such force that she fell backwards across the table. Much of the shopping ended up on the floor. Molly screamed but he was out the door and was gone.

Molly lay on the table amongst spilt milk and squashed bananas, fortunately cushioned from too much damage by the loo paper, and tried to catch her breath. 'If he was a picker,' she muttered, 'well maybe I'm not so keen on them after all. Some avenging angel!'

CHAPTER SIX

By the time Brendan got home Molly had put herself back together again. Apart from a bruise on her arm where she'd hit the edge of the table, no sign remained of the intrusion. The shopping was all in its proper place, the mess had been cleaned up and she had even remembered to feed Doris and the chooks and to make a quick pasta sauce. Nevertheless, when Brendan walked in she flew to him and threw her arms around him and burst into tears. He waited until she was calm and then extracted the whole story which did not take long.

'Why didn't you ring me?'

'You were busy.'

'Or Frank Gilroy?'

'The guy was gone, Brendan. What could Sergeant Gilroy have done? It's not like he took anything.'

'Only because you interrupted him.'

'I suppose.'

'Whatever he wanted, he'll just go looking it for it somewhere else.'

Molly nodded. 'I'm sorry. I wasn't thinking straight.'

'Well of course you weren't, you were in shock.
Lying there amongst the groceries. My poor darling, at
least you weren't hurt.'

Brendan made her some camomile tea and phoned the
good Sergeant Gilroy who felt not much could now be
achieved this evening, the miscreant could be miles
away, but he would have a word with Molly in the
morning. They then ate the pasta and opted once more
for an early night. Once in bed, sleep overcame Molly
immediately; she'd had enough excitement already. So
Brendan was forced to settle down with a crime novel
lent to him by a patient. It was gripping and swept him
along until chapter four. It was then that he realised the
young wife in the lonely farmhouse was about to open
the door to a serial killer. He did not have a good night.

For very different reasons, Pat Turner did not have a
good night either. She tossed and turned and thought
about her father and what he had become and failed, as
she had so many times before, to understand the changes
that had occurred. The trouble was, Pat still loved Artie.
In spite of his monstrous behaviour – more monstrous
even than usual today – she remembered the man he had
been before the accident. No saint, nothing like that, but
one who could laugh and show affection at least and tell
a joke and feel some sympathy for others when trouble
struck. An ordinary, decent man. A good father. She
wondered why he had been unable to accept the fate that
had befallen him with some degree of grace. Other
people did. Pat often read the death notices in the paper
and it was there all the time, mention of illness bravely
borne, of courage and humour and patience in the face of
suffering. Not Artie. Artie just wanted to kick everyone
else in the teeth, make sure they shared his pain.

He was her dad. Why couldn't he see that he was
grinding her into the ground?

Pat had received a letter the day before from an old friend, a woman she'd known since childhood. It was an invitation to stay for a week or two at a beach house in Somers. She held the letter now and prayed that a merciful god would find a way for her to go but she did not believe for a moment that it would be happen. The last sixteen years had tried Pat's faith sorely.

Brendan had already made a thorough check of the farm when Molly put breakfast on the table next morning. He'd not been able to find anything damaged, missing or out of place; there were no signs of their nocturnal visitor at all. He was still reluctant to leave Molly alone, especially when the pickers were so close by at Cameron's.

'We don't know he was a picker, Brendan. That's stereotyping,' Molly said, forgetting she'd done the same thing herself.

Brendan had to agree that it was.

'The only picker I've seen was the little boy. I don't think he's going to do much harm.'

'You know what we need? A dog.'

'Dogs are nice. But they cost money, Brendan. And they're not exactly productive.'

'I'm pretty sure on a farm they're a tax deduction.'

'You've got to earn money before you pay tax.'

'Moll, please. I'm talking about a guard dog. Something to protect you when I'm not here. A Doberman'd be good, I've always wanted a Doberman.'

'A *Doberman*? They're not very …' She couldn't find the word.

'Cuddly? No, they're not. That, my darling, is the whole point. Or we could get a gun of course. Think about it. I must go.' He went off to work. Molly decided she'd rather not to think about.

By the time he'd driven to the hospital Brendan had

become quite enamoured with the idea of a dog. A dog and a gun, and he mentioned both to Marta. She was concerned about Molly and hoped Frank Gilroy might be able to discover the identity of the intruder though it did seem unlikely. Marta shared Molly's reservations about Dobermans, she knew they needed a great deal of training and exercise and wondered when Brendan would find the time. As for guns, she was vehemently opposed to them.

'You do not need a gun, Brendan. We have police to deal with lawbreakers.'

'What if an animal gets injured?'

'Call the vet!'

'So what would you do, Marta, if someone barged in here and threatened your patients?'

'I have no idea, Brendan! I hope I would be resourceful enough – brave enough – to deal with the situation sensibly. I do know that waving a gun around is rarely a good idea!'

She was upset and Brendan backed off. 'Okay! Point taken.'

'I am sorry. But I have already seen too much killing. No guns.'

Brendan just nodded. He didn't know very much of Marta's story, only that she had come to Australia as a refugee from Hungary. He could not begin to imagine what she had been through but he thought it would certainly explain her attitude.

At the Dean house, Vicky finished a phone call. 'Thanks for the information, Mr. O'Grady, I'll be on the lookout. Might just let the doctors know as well … yes, can't be too careful. Bye, now.' She hung up.

'What?' said her mother.

'Max O'Grady, he's a vet from up near Holbrook. He's found hydatids in some sheep up there, just wanted

A COUNTRY PRACTICE

to let me know. I'll give Terence a ring later.'

'Oh, right.' Shirley was more interested in her shopping list.'

'Are you giving Frank the curry then?'

'No, I changed my mind.'

'Just as well. So what's the lucky man getting?'

'We're having Persian.'

'I see. Ever cooked Persian before, Mum?'

'Got to be a first time for everything, darling. Such an exotic cuisine. So aromatic.'

'So glad I'm going out. See you later.'

'You were such a dear little girl, I wonder what happened?'

But Vicky had gone.

Sergeant Frank Gilroy, the man who was going to dine like a Shah, had just arrived at the Jones farm and Molly, who had not taken long to learn country etiquette, was making tea and admiring the banksia rose he had brought her.

'That is so lovely of you, Sergeant Gilroy. I just adore banksias, they're so brilliant at making ugly things beautiful, don't you think?'

'Well, they're good climbers alright. I'm glad you like it. It's the yellow one.'

'My favourite colour.'

'I do need to ask you a few questions, if that's alright?'

'About the intruder? Of course. But I don't think I'm going to be much help. It all happened so quickly.'

'So you can't give me a description?'

'Not really. Medium height, thin. I'd say young from the way he moved, he was agile, you know?'

'Hair?'

'I didn't see, he had some sort of hood. Do you think he would have been a picker?'

51

'No way of knowing,' said Frank.

'Well he didn't find anything worth stealing, so I don't suppose he'll be back.'

Frank couldn't see any point in scaring her. 'No, with any luck, he's on his way to Queensland by now.' He put his notebook away. 'So how are your veggies going?'

'Well I've only got a few things in so far. Herbs and fennel and silver beet and some carrots. I've been using pig sh- manure on everything, that should give them a nudge.'

Frank was horrified. 'Oh, you mustn't do that! Not fresh manure!'

'Really, why not?'

'It's way too strong, it'll burn your seedlings. Burn anything.'

'Damn. And I've got such a lovely fresh supply.'

'Best to dig it all out. Replace it with fresh soil.'

Molly was deflated. 'One day I'll get something right.'

'Give yourself a break, love. You're just starting out. You'll get the hang of things.' But Molly's vision of herself as the self-sufficient farmer was beginning to fray at the edges.

'Hydatids?' said Terence Elliot. 'Now that *is* interesting. Where did you learn about this?' Vicky had dropped by the surgery to pass on the news. She had not expected quite such a reaction.

'A vet in Holbrook. He thinks it might be travelling with the pickers – with their dogs, that is – since they tend to move from north to south. I'll start checking the sheep around here but I thought you should know too.'

'Well it might just explain a little medical mystery. Do you think you could get some hydatid fluid for me, Vicky?'

'You want to do a Casoni test? Yes, I think I can manage that.' She wondered who the patient might be. And then Terence took a packet of jelly beans out of his desk drawer which narrowed the field a bit.

'Is this about a little boy out at Cameron's?'

'You've seen him then?'

Vicky nodded. 'I'll get you the fluid. I think you could be on to something, Terence.'

Alex Popovich was enjoying the brief respite offered by smoke-o. He was in his sixties and starting to realise that fruit-picking was no job for a man with a chronically bad back. It was an old injury from the days when he'd fought with Tito's partisans in the war-torn Balkans; he liked to tell himself that he should be used to it by now and indeed he could cope with it most of the time but today it was giving him hell. He put on a good face when he saw Silvia coming; he hoped she wasn't looking for Lexy again.

'Have you seen him, Dad?' She'd always called him Dad, ever since she and Janni had got married. It was a mark of respect, of affection. Her own father had died when she was very young; Alex had almost come to replace him. He loved her dearly but he did not want to see her throwing her life away.

'Silvia? Sit down, drink your tea. Lexy will be alright. He'll be over at that farm, there are chickens, a pig. It is safe for him to explore a little. Good for him. There are no roads to cross, just a fence to climb. He gets bored here.'

Silvia didn't sit. Her eyes kept darting around, looking for her son. 'I can't help it. I don't like him to go wandering.'

Alex wondered if she would ever relax again. She could not go on forever, wound up tight as a spring, so afraid of losing what was left. He said, as gently as he could, 'You need to look after yourself as well. For the boy's sake. Janni was my son, Silvia, I miss him too. But he is gone. He cannot be a father to Lexy. And you cannot spend your life clinging to the past.'

She knew what he was saying. But the idea of another man was more than she could contemplate. 'I'm sorry. I'll just have a quick look for him. You're right – he's probably at the farm.'

Silvia did not find Lexy straight away but she saw someone in purple overalls and thought she had probably found his weird lady. It was indeed Molly, digging up a corner of the vegetable patch where she intended to plant radishes, of which Brendan was inordinately fond. Molly did not see Silvia approach at first, she was concentrating on the job in hand and humming that song from 'Evita' to herself. But she looked up and smiled when Silvia's shadow fell over her. 'Self-sufficiency is hard work, don't let anyone tell you otherwise. What can I do for you?'

Silvia smiled back, a little uncertainly. 'I'm looking for my son.'

'Skinny kid? About five, curly hair?'

'That's Lexy.'

'He was certainly here yesterday. I'm Molly Jones, by the way, shall we have a look for him?'

'Silvia Popovich. I don't want to interrupt you.'

'I'm glad you did, it was killing me. He's okay, is he, Lexy?

'What do you mean?'

'Oh, just that he was so hungry!' Molly laughed but went on more seriously. 'And he's very thin, isn't he?'

Silvia was defensive. 'I do feed him! The best food I can manage. Little boys are always hungry, do you have any of your own?'

'No, not yet. And please – I wasn't being critical. I just thought he'd maybe had an illness, that's all.'

'No.' She hesitated, she almost went on but then she changed the subject. 'You run this place on your own, do you?'

'Well – mostly. My husband's a nurse at the hospital. We haven't been here long. Got a lot to learn.'

Silvia looked around and nodded as though she agreed with that. 'I'd give anything for a place of my own. But my husband's dead. There's just me and my father-in-law and Lexy. You can't save much picking fruit.'

'I'm sure it must be very hard. Oh, look. Isn't that Lexy over by the pig pen?'

'Sounds right. He's mad about animals.'

Lexy was sitting on the ground outside Doris's pen, hunched over and holding his stomach. He looked up, worried, when they approached, as though he thought he might be in trouble. 'I just came to see the pig, Mummy.'

'It's alright, darling. Is your tummy hurting?'

The child nodded. Silvia put out a hand and helped him to his feet. 'Come on then. We'll get some bi-carb, that'll make it feel better.' She turned to Molly. 'It happens now and then, it's nothing serious.'

Molly nodded and forced a smile. She wasn't convinced. 'See you again, then. Let Lexy come if he wants to, he's welcome any time.'

'That's nice of you. Thanks.'

Molly watched them go, concerned about the child, going through the possibilities in her head. All she could think of was appendicitis. The mother, Silvia, was concerned too, Molly was sure of that. She felt sorry for her, sorry that she'd upset her. She'd talk to Brendan about the kid, maybe he'd have some ideas.

CHAPTER SEVEN

Vicky was pursuing her own line of enquiry out at Bill
Ferguson's farm. Bill had watched her car come up the
drive and was pleased as always to see her. Vicky had
been one of those who'd given quiet support when
Kerry-Anne walked out; she'd find some veterinary
excuse to pop in and say g'day and made sure she had
time to stay on for coffee and a chat. Those had been
hard days and Bill had wanted to stay in bed and pull the
blankets over his head but you can't do that with a mob
of cows waiting to be milked.

Privately Vicky thought that Bill was better off
without Kerry-Anne, except for that fact that he'd
worshipped the ground the silly girl walked on. Kerry-
Anne, who seemed to think that being a farmer's wife
meant lolling about on a hay bale looking decorative,
had been of no assistance to Bill whatsoever that Vicky
could see, except perhaps in bed, and even there she'd
failed to provide him with any kids. The ever-practical
Vicky was of the commonly-held opinion that young
farmers should not marry airheads like Kerry-Anne but

nurses or school-teachers or maybe accountants; women with a brain in their heads who could earn a living off the property in the drought years. That was the ideal. (It was interesting that she never included vets in the list.)

'So how've you been?' she enquired now.

'Yeah, not too bad,' said Bill, lying, because he was suffering from a bout of cystitis, had not been taking the medication Terence prescribed and was starting to feel the consequences.

'I've just been next door to the Walters', it's all locked up. You wouldn't know where they are?'

Bill smiled. 'I can help you with that alright. Shelley went into labour late yesterday, she's a few weeks early so they took her straight to Burrigan. But apparently it's all going okay.'

'Oh, that's great. That explains it.'

'Tom Shepherd's keeping an eye on things for them.'

'The aptly named Tom. I might have a word to him, then.' She grinned. 'Or I could just trespass.'

'So what's up?'

'I got a report of hydatids in sheep up around Holbrook. I want to make some checks, see if we've got a problem.'

'Well Sid won't mind if you take a look at his flock. I'll tell him next time he rings.'

'Thanks, Bill. I'd hate any rumours to get around that I was stealing his prize ram. You can imagine what Esme Watson'd make of it.'

They laughed and he waved her off. He would have offered to help but he was feeling too crook and he still had to get through the milking.

Bill was not the only one having a bad day but at least his illness was curable. Emily Page was not so fortunate. Doctors, Terence Elliott amongst them, had told her that people with rheumatoid arthritis could live to a ripe old age. They did not discuss whether that option would have much appeal, especially in 1981 when treatments for the disease were limited. Emily was finding the constant pain and the sleepless nights hard to endure; harder still was the thought that soon she would need help just to shower and dress and make a cup of tea.

She surveyed the remains of her grandmother's Royal Doulton sugar bowl, lying smashed on the floor. She had barely felt it slip through her fingers. She tried to laugh, she thought her daughter Laura would probably be glad the damn thing was broken, but tears came instead. She wondered how on earth she would manage to sweep it up then remembered that her cleaning lady was coming. When she had composed herself, she scrunched her way slowly through the spilt sugar to the phone and rang Shirley Dean to make an appointment.

'We can fit you in after lunch, Emily, say one-thirty? But it might have to be Simon. Terence is out rushing around the countryside.'

'Not a problem, Shirley, I've already met young Dr. Bowen, he'll do nicely.'

Shirley was surprised by that but let it pass. 'How will you get here, are you up to driving?'

'Oh, I'll manage,' said Emily, who knew she wasn't up to it at all but hated to make a fuss.

'Hang on just a minute, could you?' said Shirley and went to ask Simon if he could fit in a house call before afternoon surgery. Simon was agreeable and then positively eager when Shirley passed on Emily's message that she looked forward to meeting Charlie Bowen's grandson.

'She didn't tell me she knew Grandie when I dropped her parcel in. Where on earth did those two meet?'

'I've no idea,' said Shirley, 'none at all.' They were equally bewildered.

***

Terence could have enlightened them but he had other things on his mind. He actually felt a little uncomfortable; a doctor can hardly accost a small child at an apple orchard and demand an examination. The matter required a degree of delicacy. Fortunately, the child in question accosted Terence – or rather, nearly bowled him over when he came rushing out from between the trees and came to an abrupt halt in front of him.

'Whoa, there! It's Lexy, isn't it? Is your mummy around?'

Lexy just stared at him. Then Silvia came rushing up. 'What do you want, who are you?' She put protective hands on Lexy's shoulders.

'My name's Terence Elliot, I'm a doctor. You're Lexy's mother?' She nodded. 'I wanted a quick word with you, Mrs -?'

'Popovich, Silvia Popovich. What about?' She was upset, defensive. Terence thought perhaps she often was.

'Please … I don't want to alarm you. But I was out here yesterday, seeing a couple of patients. And I happened to notice Lexy. And since then we've received some information, medical information. The thing is, Mrs Popovich, Lexy could have quite a serious illness. Can you tell me how he eats, how he sleeps?'

'Just fine. There's nothing wrong with him. I don't know what you're talking about!'

Alex had noticed the altercation from where he was picking further down the row and had quietly joined them with a nod to Terence, who continued. 'He's showing certain symptoms, Mrs. Popovich. It could be nothing. It could be serious. A quick test at the hospital would show us one way or the other.' Silvia was shaking her head. 'Does he ever get stomach pains?'

'No!' Silvia was vehement.

'Yes,' said Alex quietly. 'Often. Sometimes he wakes

in the night with the pain.'

Terence looked at Lexy who gave a tiny nod but Silvia seemed to feel betrayed. Terence was gentle. 'It's a very simple test, Mrs Popovich. Quite harmless. You could be with Lexy while we did it.'

'And if this test is positive?'

'We can treat the disease. Cure it.'

'Then you must take the boy. Silvia, he's your son. My grandson. We must keep him well, you know we must.'

Silvia gave in then and nodded. Lexy looked up at her, fearful. 'It'll be alright, darling,' Silvia said without conviction.

Alex and Terence exchanged a glance.

'You'll come with us, Mr. Popovich?'

'I think I should keep picking if Silvia can manage. Mr Cameron is … tough, you know.'

'Yes, I do know. I could have a word to him.'

'Lexy and I will manage,' said Silvia. 'I'll get my keys. Can I follow you, Dr. Elliott?'

'Of course.'

While she was gone, Alex said to Terence, 'What is it you suspect?'

'Hydatids, Mr. Popovich. Are you familiar with it?'

'I have heard of it. But why do you think Lexy …?'

'That little pot belly of his. It's often a symptom. But I could be wrong.'

'At least we will know.'

At the hospital, they found Vicky preparing a syringe. Terence introduced her and Silvia was bewildered to find that a vet was involved in the test. Vicky tried to explain in words that Lexy might understand; how these tiny little tapeworms, just millimetres long, were found in many animals; how they formed cysts and how sterilised fluid from the cysts could actually be used to test for their presence in people. She could see that both Lexy and even Silvia were totally lost.

'They're called hydatids,' Terence said, hoping that might help.

Silvia said, 'Oh, I've heard of those! But aren't they found in meat that isn't properly cooked? And I'm really careful about things like that!'

'I'm sure you are, Mrs. Popovich.' Terence was quick to calm her.

Vicky went on. 'The thing is, hydatids were found in some sheep a bit to the north where fruit pickers were working. It's the dogs that are the problem. If they ate infected meat and Lexy played with them he could have picked it up that way. However it happened, it's not your fault.'

'If it happened at all. First we need to do this test.'

'So if it does come up positive, what then? Do I give him a dose of worm medicine?' Vicky and Terence exchanged a glance. Terence decided to beat around the bush a little.

'It's a little more complicated than that, Mrs. Popovich. Let's just wait and see, shall we? Now you're a brave boy, Lexy, I can tell that – but I do have to put a little needle into your hand. Would a jelly bean help?'

Lexy could barely nod but he took the jelly bean and Terence chattered away. 'Now if the test is positive, we'll see a rash on Lexy's arm within half an hour or so. If there's no rash, he's clear, nothing worry about. Okay?'

The needle went in. Lexy winced but didn't cry out. 'There we go ... all done.' Terence beamed reassuringly on mother and son.

'What next?' asked Silvia.

'We'll find someone to make you a cup of tea,' said Vicky. 'I'll attend to that, I could do with one myself.' And she left.

'All you have to do is sit and relax for a bit,' said Terence.

'What I meant,' said Silvia, 'was what if it's positive?'

Terence tried to keep his tone light, to make it all sound like no big deal. 'Well that means the worms could have formed a cyst on Lexy's liver. Which we'd remove with a very simple operation. This hydatids thing – it's not some rare, exotic disease. It's quite common, especially in the country. It's nothing to worry about.' He turned to Lexy. 'But I think we should wait and see how the test goes, don't you? And have another jelly bean.' He took one himself and gave the little packet to Lexy. 'I'll be back soon.' He left them, concerned by the look of fear on Silvia's face.

In Marta's office he was about to phone Simon when he saw Brendan pass in the corridor bearing a tray. 'For our Casoni test people?' Brendan nodded. 'You're just the man, Brendan. See if you can get them to relax a bit? If it's positive, the mum's going to be difficult, I think.'

'That was Vicky's feeling too. What's the problem?'

'No idea. Maybe she doesn't like hospitals.' Which was a lot closer to the truth that Terence could have imagined.

Emily Page was not fond of hospitals. Though she could see they had their place in the scheme of things, the thought that her illness could lead to a protracted stay in one filled her with dread. She was determined to do whatever she could to ward off the evil day. It helped to see Simon Bowen come walking up her path. Helped, because the sight of him made her feel young again. In spite of the pain, Emily couldn't help smiling.

As she went to answer the doorbell, she noticed a certain photo on the hall-stand and quickly whisked it out of sight. That would have given the game away immediately and she was hoping to have a little fun with Simon. She ushered him in. 'So good of you to make a house call, Simon.'

'I told you. All part of the service.'

It was, at first, a normal consultation. They discussed Emily's medication, anti-inflammatories and pain-killers, neither of which seemed to be doing what was required.

'I see you did try cyclophosamide a few years ago.'

'The cure was worse than the disease.'

'A lot of people find it hard to tolerate. Was it the nausea?'

Emily nodded. 'And the fact that half my hair fell out. Which may not seem so important to a man –'

Simon smiled. 'You wouldn't believe the number of men who come asking about a cure for baldness. Of course it's important, you need to feel good about yourself. Well then. We can give you something stronger for the pain. And increase the Indocid. Are you sleeping?'

'Old women don't need much sleep, Simon. I read.'

'Rheumatoid arthritis is an auto-immune disease, Emily. As you know. Your body's at war with itself. You *do* need sleep. I think a mild sedative now and then might help quite a lot.'

Emily sighed. 'I'm going to rattle. But perhaps you're right.'

Simon was busy writing out prescriptions. 'Would you like me to drop these off at the pharmacy? Get them to deliver?'

'That would be a great help.'

'It's a pleasure. Now tell me, how did you know my grandfather?'

'Oh dear. Charlie Bowen and I. Where *did* we meet? I fear it's lost in the mists of antiquity.'

'I don't believe you, Emily. You've both still got all

your marbles, you're not that old.' Emily just smiled enigmatically. 'Were you a nurse?'

'Me?' She laughed. 'Not really. Well. In a way, I suppose.'

'You're not going to tell me, are you?'

'Not yet. Then your curiosity might force you to pay me another visit. Please do, I enjoy the company of young people.'

'Thank you. Of course I'll come. And you're quite right, I'm dying to know about you and Grandie!' He closed his bag but they talked for a while longer before Simon realised he'd be late for the afternoon clinic and reluctantly took his leave. 'Don't get up, I can see myself out. Goodbye, Emily.

'Goodbye, Simon. Thank you again. Oh, and tell Terence we simply must do something to rescue Pat Turner.' Simon was about to query this but she shook her head. 'Just tell him.'

'Right.' He went then. After the door closed behind him, Emily walked painfully to the hall-stand again and took the photo out of the drawer where she'd hidden it. She stared at it for a long time. It showed an army officer and an army nurse, smiling in the sunlight somewhere in Egypt. The man looked remarkably like Simon Bowen.

CHAPTER EIGHT

Simon himself returned to the surgery to find it still locked up after the lunch break. Shirley however was only moments behind him. She'd dashed home for half an hour to continue preparations for her Persian dinner.

'You're very welcome to join us, you know, you and Vicky.' Simon declined. 'You don't like Persian? Or you want the chance to race off my daughter?'

'Shirl!'

'Oh you know me, darling. Good luck, I say.'

'And you think I'll need it.'

'To be honest, yes.'

'Changing the subject,' said Simon, 'is there any news on the little boy with hydatids? If indeed he has hydatids?'

'Not a word. Terence knew I was going home – and he knew you'd be at Emily's. Nothing on the answering machine either.'

'Oh well. Maybe it came up negative after all.'

But the fact was that nobody knew. When Brendan had arrived to deliver tea and juice and good cheer to

Silvia and Lexy, they were nowhere to be found. A quick search of the hospital grounds soon revealed that Silvia's car had gone. Terence and Vicky dithered, wondering where to look for them and decided to go first to the orchard and talk to Alex Popovich.

They found him easily enough and explained the situation. Alex was upset. 'What did you tell Silvia about this disease?'

'We explained what it was and how the test worked. She wanted to know what would happen if it was positive so I told her. If Lexy had a cyst we could remove it with a simple operation.'

'Surgery. In an operating theatre.'

'Well yes.'

'And this is necessary?'

'Mr Popovich,' said Vicky gently, 'without it, he could die.'

'I understand. But you must both understand too. Lexy's father, Janni – he became ill and went to hospital and died on the operating table. We were told almost nothing. This wall of silence comes down. Maybe a mistake. Maybe not. But no one talks to us. So Silvia – she does not trust hospitals, she fears them.'

Terence was shattered. 'I do understand. And I'm so sorry. I went barging in … I've made a mess of it.'

'You were trying to help my grandson.' He sighed. 'The apples will have to wait. I think they will be at the camp park.'

Silvia was dismayed when they arrived at the cabin. Lexy cowered at the back of it and would not come out.

'How could you bring them here, Dad? How could you! Lexy is terrified, all he can talk about is worms in his tummy. And I – you think I would let them operate?'

'You want him to die, Silvia? Is that what you want?' Alex's voice was sharp. Terence realised that he too had his fears. Silvia stared at her father-in-law, shocked, and he was instantly contrite. 'I'm sorry, I didn't meant to shout. But Silvie, we must be brave. Please. Let the doctor look at Lexy's arm.'

She broke down then, sobbing. 'I have looked … it's all red.'

Vicky moved past them then and went to Lexy and sat on the bed beside him. 'Lexy, I'm a vet, right? So I know a bit about animals. All sorts of animals. Do you know we've all got lots of things that live inside us? Like worms and bacteria in our gut. And some of them are good guys that keep us healthy and some of them are bad. The little worms you've got are bad. So we need to get rid of them. Alright?'

Lexy stared at the floor.

Vicky ploughed on. 'You'll learn more about these things when you go to school, it's really quite interesting. But it's nothing to be afraid of because it happens to everyone sometime or other. Okay?'

Lexy looked up at her then, eyes wide. 'Will you stay with me at the hospital?'

'Sure. If you'd like that.'

Terence flashed her a look of gratitude and turned to Silvia. 'Mrs. Popovich?' Silvia took a deep breath. Her hands were clenched but she nodded.

Simon had seldom been so glad of an interruption. Naturally he wasn't glad that a small boy had a hydatid cyst and needed surgery but really, he thought, any excuse to terminate his current consultation was a gift from some guardian angel.

His patient was a seventeen-year-old called Sheree Smallwood, whom Simon had already upset by calling Cheryl. Sheree was the third seventeen-year-old to make an appointment with Simon in the past two weeks. He suspected they might all know each other; might all be students at Burrigan High or something like that, but he couldn't be sure. They each appeared to have a giant schoolgirl crush on Simon and he had no idea how to handle the situation in a suitably professional manner. They were all unfortunately old enough to make appointments to see him without a parent and when they came, each had some vague complaint involving indefinable aches and pains and fevers. He was pretty sure the symptoms were invented – but then what if he ignored them and one turned out to be real and he missed something fatal like encephalitis? Cheryl, for instance, no Sheree damn it, *Sheree* was complaining of headaches and nausea (meningitis?) while constantly batting her eyelashes at him and thrusting her small but perfectly formed breasts as far forward as they would go.

'Oh, doctor,' she said. 'I feel so awfully unwell. I'm worried I might have something really *serious*.' The eyelashes went mad. 'But of course I have absolute faith in you.'

And that is when Shirley rang through to say Simon was needed at the hospital.

'I don't think there's anything to worry about, Sheree. Paracetamol every four hours. But no more than eight a day, of course. Early nights and drink plenty of fluids. Come back if you're not feeling better. I'm so sorry I've got to dash, emergency.'

Simon was gone, leaving Sheree to dream of amazing scenarios if only she had been the emergency.

Given the fact that his small patient had eaten no lunch, and very much afraid the courage of both mother and son would fail them at any moment, Terence and Simon had decided to proceed with the surgery that afternoon. Lexy was already prepped and on a trolley. Silvia clung to his hand, even while Vicky, gowned for theatre, held on to the other one. Anxiety was writ so large on Silvia's face that Terence was quite sure they had made the right decision.

'You'll be fine, darling, it'll be alright.' Silvia spoke without conviction. Lexy didn't respond. 'Can't he talk?'

Brendan explained. 'He's had his pre-op medication, Mrs. Popovich. It's made him very sleepy, that's all. He's just about out to it. Vicky and I will look after him, promise. Here we go now.'

Alex put a hand on Silvia's shoulder, forcing himself to keep calm as the doors opened and Lexy disappeared through them. They shut behind him with a gentle thud. Silvia shuddered.

'It was just like that, Dad. The same doors, the same noise …'

'Come,' he said. 'Come and sit down.' He led her away down the corridor to where there were some seats.

'I never said goodbye. And he never same back.'

'This time will be different. They are good people looking after Lexy. Nothing bad will happen.'

'That's what we thought when they took Janni away.'

Alex sighed. 'Silvie. I miss him too. Every day. But you cannot spend your life in the past. For Lexy's sake, you have to pick up the pieces and move on. I sometimes think …' He trailed off.

'What?'

'You might do it more easily if I were not here. I feel I am a burden.'

'No! No, please. Don't ever say that. You do more than your share. We need you, Dad.'

'Then we must all of us make an effort. Try to be – not so sad? So worried about the future. It is good to laugh sometimes. And I will say it again – Lexy must start school and learn about the world.' He smiled, he tried to make a little joke. 'About the bugs, you know, like Vicky said.'

'I'm glad he's not at school now. Hydatids, imagine. The kids would have given him hell.'

Alex shook his head. 'They are not like that these days, Silvia. Kids are much smarter. They all get nits, they think it's a joke. Not shameful.'

She thought, how would he know? She wished he wouldn't talk about school. She wished he wouldn't hint that she should find another man, a father for Lexy. She knew he was right but she didn't want to go there, to close the door on the past. She wanted things to stay as they had been. 'When this is over. We'll talk about it then, Dad. Let's get today over?'

Alex could only nod. There was never a good time to talk about the future.

In the theatre, Terence had already begun Lexy's surgery with Vicky, there to fulfil her promise, as an interested observer. The incision to get to the liver was simple enough and the cause of Lexy's problem soon became clear: a large cyst right on the surface.

'Get a bit closer, Vicky, if you want.' Vicky moved in for a good look. In fact they were all – Simon, Marta, Brendan – keen to see.

'Gosh, it's big.'

'Quite a size,' Terence agreed. 'Dissecting forceps.' Marta passed them and soon after the curved scissors. Vicky, who had never seen Terence operate, was amazed at the skill and speed with which he worked.

'Only problem,' Terence said, 'is to make sure we get it out in one piece.'

'Or what?' It was Brendan who asked.

'If it's broken then it can spread – brain, lungs, back to the liver. Nasty.' There was tension while he proceeded to cut the cyst out. 'How's it going at your end, Simon?'

'Yes, good. Blood pressure and pulse both fine.'

A few moments passed and then Terence lifted the

cyst out and popped it in a kidney dish.

'There we go. One hydatid cyst safely taken into custody.' The dish was passed to Brendan who was scout and he and Vicky peered at it while Terence and Marta finished off.

'I bet young Lexy would like to see it when he wakes up,' Brendan said but Terence pointed out that the cyst had to be dissected and investigated. Vicky thought it was a bit gross anyway but Brendan and Simon laughed. 'That's the point,' said Simon. 'If you'd ever been a small boy, you'd understand.'

Vicky was reminded if not of the cyst exactly, then certainly of things gross, sometime later at home. Having dressed for her dinner with Simon, she appeared in the kitchen to find that Frank had already arrived. She greeted him warmly; no one deserved what Frank was about to endure.

'Has Mum told you what you're in for, Frank?'

'Persian, I believe.'

'I was saying I hope it's not too exotic for Frank.'

'And I told your mother I eat just about anything.'

'Just as well,' said Vicky. 'So what's on the menu, Mum?'

Shirley ran through it. 'We're having eggplant dip, and then head-and-hoof soup, followed by kebabs with —'

'Hold it, *what* soup?'

'It's sheep. You make it with —'

'On second thoughts, I don't think I want to know, do you, Frank?'

'I'm sure it's very nutritious,' said Frank loyally.

'What's this, exactly?' Vicky was peering into a bowl of unidentified round objects the size of ping pong balls. 'Do you know what it is, Frank?' Frank looked as though he'd rather not be put on the spot. 'Sheep's eyes, perhaps?' Vicky offered. 'Left over from the soup?'

'Horrible child, it's falafel,' said Shirley. 'They're little spiced balls of chickpea that's ground –'

'I know what falafel is, Mum. I've just never seen any that looked like that before.'

'My own special recipe. Delicious.' Shirley changed the subject. 'That's a new dress, isn't it?'

'Yeah. Molly made it for me.'

'She's a clever girl, it suits you, doesn't it suit her, Frank?'

'Very nice,' said Frank. 'I'm sure Dr Bowen will think so as well.'

'Well I hope so,' said Vicky. 'I'd like to show him that even us country yokels can scrub up okay. Any other treats in store, Mum?'

'Lots of things, you don't know what you're missing.'

'A case of salmonella poisoning probably. Health insurance up to date, is it, Frank?'

'You see what I have to put up with, Frank? Be a dear, pour me some wine.'

'Pour us all one,' said Vicky. 'Simon won't be here for at least half an hour. And tell me, any more word on the intruder?'

Frank was dutifully opening a bottle of wine while he watched Shirley inexpertly chop coriander.

'No, nothing. Either he's gone or he's keeping a low profile. Shirl, are you sure you wouldn't like me to do that? I'm quite good at chopping things.'

'Part of the job description, isn't it, Frank?'

Shirley thought that maybe Vicky was a tad nervous about this date with Simon. Or maybe she just had the devil in her tonight. Probably the latter. Her daughter got like that sometimes. As for Frank, he told himself he liked smart women or he wouldn't be standing in this kitchen. He passed the wine. 'Here's to a pleasant evening,' he said, ever the peacemaker.

***

Simon and Terence's evening had started pleasantly enough, with a debrief in Terence's study after Lexy's surgery. Simon was drinking mineral water, since he'd be driving later on. The operation had gone well and they both knew it; Simon was getting to expect nothing less from Terence but the expertise, even artistry of the man still surprised him. But he managed to limit himself to just one question.

'Have you actually done it before then? A cyst removal?'

'What, a hydatid cyst? No, hardly. I lied to Silvia Popovich, you don't see them often at all. But I did know the important thing was to get it out whole. And we somehow managed that. So Lexy should make a full recovery.' He swirled his malt around in the glass. 'If his mother doesn't smother him to death.'

'Not an easy life, you told me that.'

'True, but I don't think she's the sort to let hard work bother her.'

'So what's her problem?'

'Loss. It's made her fearful and over-protective. That's my guess, anyway.'

Simon smiled and shook his head.

'What?' Terence asked.

'This is why you like it, isn't it? Working in the country, in a small hospital, a small practice. Can you imagine in the city, sitting around talking about patients like this? Wondering how you could help them? Especially can you imagine a surgeon doing it? I mean, it just wouldn't happen, you'd be lucky if you remembered their name.'

'Right on all counts. It's like a conveyor belt. Here you get to treat the whole person. So much more interesting.'

Simon grinned. 'Be warned then. I have a message for

you from Emily Page. 'Tell Terence we simply must do something to rescue Pat Turner.' Make sense?'

Terence sighed. 'Unfortunately, it makes perfect sense. How did you get on with Emily, anyway?'

'I wish we could do more to help her as well. She's in a bad way. But she's a brave woman. I think she's fascinating. Charming. And I think she quite likes me.' He got up. 'I just hope the same can be said about my dinner date. Wish me luck.' He paused at the door. 'I suppose you were aware that Emily knew my grandfather.'

'I think I did hear something.'

'Which you have no intention of enlarging on.'

'Up to Emily, wouldn't you say?'

'Hm. Time I gave Grandie a ring, he's got a birthday coming up.' And Simon left an amused Terence to his Islay malt.

CHAPTER NINE

'*Polo*?' said Vicky, who was not amused in the least. 'You can't be serious!'

The evening had started off well. Simon thought she looked terrific in the new dress and said so. He'd brought her here to the restaurant at Hicklewhite's Winery where, it turned out, she'd been wanting to come for ages. And they'd had a most interesting, if not exactly romantic discussion about parasitic diseases – in sheep, in humans, even in fish. This had not put either of them off their entrée of rainbow trout stuffed with crab. And then Vicky had asked Simon about his recent weekend with his cousins, the Smythe-Kings, and Simon unwisely mentioned that they'd asked him to join the polo club. As Shirley had known it would – but had failed to warn him – a distinct chill descended over the table.

'What's wrong with polo?'

'Oh, Simon! It's so … you know.'

'No, I don't know.'

'Just look at the sort of people who play it! Upper-class wankers with private school accents and over-loaded bank accounts.'

Simon took umbrage at that. 'I hope you're not describing me, Victoria. My bank account tends to be over-drawn.'

'I was not including you. Not yet, anyway. But I do think it's a game for a rather snobby clique. It costs too much to be anything else, I'm amazed you can afford it.'

'I wouldn't have to buy my own ponies.'

'Got a stable full, have they, your cousins?' It was just as well the waiter arrived to top up their glasses.

The ambience at the Jones' place was decidedly more down market, the atmosphere much warmer. Molly and Brendan were having a beer on the back verandah. The evening sounds of the country wafted up to them; the gentle lowing of cows released from milking, the reliable put-put of an old tractor heading home, Doris snuffling in her pen. However, they too were talking parasites.

'Do pigs get hydatids?' Molly asked.

'I think so.'

'Poor Doris. I must be careful what she eats. And keep her away from dogs.'

'When we get a dog it'll be de-wormed regularly. I do think Doris is pretty safe.'

'I bet Silvia thought Lexy was pretty safe.'

Brendan shook his head. 'Silvia doesn't know how to feel safe.'

'Then we'll have to teach her,' said Molly, thereby getting on board with a growing number of people for whom the Popovich family's welfare was suddenly a high priority.

The family in question knew nothing of this. Alex was now back at the camping ground having a shower and a quick meal. At the hospital, Marta arrived to do Lexy's obs and found an anxious Silvia sitting by his bed.

'He's still unconscious, Matron. Shouldn't he be awake by now?'

'He's doing fine. The anaesthetic's just about worn off and he's sleeping normally. I wouldn't be surprised if he slept through the night.'

'You're quite sure?'

'Absolutely. Dr Elliott told you – the operation was a complete success.'

Silvia did not seem reassured. 'He's such a little boy …'

'Children always seem so vulnerable. But really, they are very much stronger than we think. It's you I'm worried about, Mrs. Popovich. Why don't you go home and get some sleep? We'll look after Lexy.'

'I couldn't do that. What if he woke up and I wasn't here? He'd be so frightened.'

Marta, who knew all about loss and understood Silvia, realised she would never win this battle. 'Alright. I'll have some sandwiches sent in. And you can use the other bed. But promise me you'll try to get some rest? We don't want another patient on our hands.'

'You are very kind.'

Marta smiled. 'Tea? Or coffee?'

'Oh tea, please. Alex – my father-in-law – drinks coffee all the time but he is European like you, Matron.'

'Where is he from?'

'Serbia. Well. It was Yugoslavia then. And you?'

'Hungary. Another world. We are fortunate to be here.'

'That's what Dad says.

'I'll see about the tea.'

Shirley's Persian dinner was progressing beautifully. That is, it was proceeding as planned. There was rather too much garlic in the eggplant dip. The falafel were like rock cakes only harder. And then Shirley put the soup tureen on the table. 'This is called kaleh pacheh,' she said brightly. 'I'm not quite sure how you serve it …'

Frank rose to his feet gallantly. 'The famous soup? Maybe I can help.'

'Oh, would you?'

Frank took the lid off the tureen and stared at the sheep's head floating within on a greasy sea of onions and chickpeas. He sat down again abruptly. 'Shirl, you won't mind my saying – I think you're supposed to take the meat off the sheep's head and return it to the broth. And then serve it.'

'Oh. Oh, I see! Silly me.'

'Never mind. Those kebabs smell wonderful, why don't we have those?'

But rather than being wonderful, the kebabs were inedible, so overcooked it was impossible to detach them from their skewers. The rice meant to accompany them stuck to the bottom of the saucepan and that was the only authentically Persian thing about the whole wretched meal.

Shirley's stoicism was nothing short of heroic.

'I'm so terribly sorry, Frank. But I can't pretend any longer. I'm the world's worst cook. And the harder I try, the more hopeless I become. You simply have to face it. To live with me would be to die of malnutrition. Or food poisoning just as Vicky suggested. A fate worse than death. I should have warned you. I apologise most sincerely.'

'Oh, Shirley. No need for any of that.' He beamed at her warmly. Shirley was alarmed.

'What do you mean?'

'I'll let you into a little secret. Alma was a terrible cook too. But not to worry. I just went off and did a course, found I really enjoyed it.'

'I know you're joking, Frank. You have to be joking.' Because if he weren't she'd have to do something unthinkable.

'Not at all. Did the whole cordon bleu thing.' He got up and went to the fridge. 'It's going to be great having someone to cook for again. Now let's see … oh, you've got some chicken pieces … mushrooms … how about I whip up a nice little Marengo, that's quick and easy.'

Shirley started looking around for a large, sharp knife. But Frank had already commandeered the most suitable. She had to settle for another pinot noir. And another.

Meanwhile, out at the winery, Simon and Vicky had left the subject of polo for what should have been safer ground. They were discussing Terence Elliott and his unexpected skills as a surgeon.

'I wonder why he gave it up for so long,' said Vicky. 'It was only that emergency Caesar, wasn't it, a few weeks ago, that got him back into the theatre?'

'So your mum said.'

'I suppose you think he's completely wasted here.'

'Not really. Mainly, I just envy his expertise. I know I'll never have the chance to acquire it.'

'Surgery's not everything, Simon. What's wrong with being a really good GP?'

'That's what Terence keeps saying.'

'Not glamorous enough?'

'Don't be ridiculous. It's more about job satisfaction.'

'I'd have thought you'd make a great GP.'

Simon shrugged. 'It has its moments. Most of the time it's really frustrating. Like this afternoon … I went to see a patient who's in constant pain and there's not a lot we can do for her. Drugs and more drugs that don't help a great deal.'

'Emily Page.'

'I can't say.'

'You don't have to. I've seen her this week as well. She's worried about what will happen to her cat when she can't look after it.'

'She's an amazing woman. So – gracious, that's the word. And such a tease. You know, she knew my grandfather? Not that she'd say where or when. I got the distinct impression there was something just a tiny bit untoward about it. I intend to find out.'

'Ah, the rattle of skeletons in the family cupboard.'

'Irresistible.' He topped up her glass with the last of the wine. 'Shame to waste it. And would you believe she plays mahjong? We're going to have a game one evening.'

Vicky spluttered into her glass. 'Polo and mahjong? Good God, Simon, what next? Charades and fox-hunting?'

'Have you ever played mahjong?'

'No.'

'It's a game of strategy, skill and calculation. I could teach you if you like. I'm sure you'd be very good.'

'I bet you drink sherry while you play, do you? I think I'll pass.' She knew she was being awful but she couldn't help it. She smiled and raised her glass. 'It was a lovely dinner though, I wonder what poor Frank had to put up with?'

Simon thought probably much the same sort of brush off that he'd got, though with worse food.

At the Dean house, Frank had finished the washing up and was making coffee. Shirley, who had found the evening emotionally draining, was trying to recover her equilibrium under her pyramid. It was not helping, she still had thoughts of homicide buzzing around in her head. Frank was concerned.

'You look a bit stressed, Shirl, I hope you didn't find my food disagreeable.'

'Good heavens no, Frank, it was marvellous. Truly amazing.'

'Pyramid not helping, then?'

'Not really, no.'

'Maybe you need a medicinal brandy.'

Shirley abandoned the pyramid immediately. 'Frank, you're a genius. Brandy! What an excellent idea!' She found the bottle and Frank poured the coffee just as Simon and Vicky arrived.

'Ah, you're back,' said Frank. 'Care to join us for coffee?'

'Or brandy?'

Simon and Vicky opted for coffee. Vicky kicked her shoes off and flopped on the couch. 'So how was dinner?'

'Oh, the chicken Marengo was alright, wasn't it, Shirl? Though your dried herbs are all a bit stale. But the soufflé really needed an eighty percent chocolate, it's always a bit insipid with anything less. I'll just put some more coffee on.' He disappeared into the kitchen, followed by Simon who was fascinated to find that Frank was apparently a fellow chef. Vicky stared at her mother in disbelief.

'*What?*'

'He just adores having someone to cook for. And he's very good.'

'That's lovely, Mum.' Shirley gave her death stare. Vicky giggled. 'Sorry. But it is funny.'

'How was your night?' asked her mother.

'Did you know he plays polo?'

'Nothing more dashing than a man on a horse.'

'I think I'll join you in a brandy after all.'

CHAPTER TEN

There were one or two sore heads in Wandin Valley next morning but not at the Jones farm and just as well; it was still dark when Brendan took Molly a cup of tea before leaving for work.

'Is it the big day?' he asked. 'Are you sure you can manage?'

Molly shook her head. 'Gary can't make it with Landrace Huntington till tomorrow. But I thought I'd get Doris all ready. Give her a bath, paint her toenails.'

With Molly you could never be sure if she were joking or not. 'Well you girls have a nice time together.'

'She'll be her usual grumpy self.'

'Not like my sweet Molly.' Brendan kissed her and was very tempted to get back into bed. But duty called. 'Love you,' he said.

'Love you too.'

He blew her another kiss and left.

'Say hello to Lexy for me! And drive carefully!' Molly called after him. She hated him going off in the dark. She couldn't forget Bob Hatfield's words after the accident that had claimed Elaine Mackay's life a few weeks earlier. *'Country roads,'* he'd said. *'Got to be careful all the time.'*

But Brendan got to work safely and found Silvia Popovich in much the same position as Marta had left her the night before, sitting by Lexy's bed. If she had lain down to sleep at all, there was no evidence of it. The night nurse had warned him what to expect and Brendan agreed with her summation – the son was doing a lot better than the mother. Silvia was holding Lexy's hand, forcing herself to stay awake. He murmured in his sleep and she quickly leant forward to stroke his forehead and reassure him.

'It's alright, darling. Mummy's here. Everything's alright. Mummy loves you very much.'

He tossed his head from side to side once or twice. Silvia became distressed. 'I'm so sorry, Lexy. I should have noticed you were sick. A good mummy would have seen that …' She started to cry. Brendan felt it was time to make his presence known.

'Hey, come on, it's going to be okay, Mrs. Popovich, really it is.'

'He's in pain. Tossing around like that.'

'You know, he's probably just having a dream?'

'I never noticed he was sick. I'm not there for him enough.' There were more tears. Brendan thought, she's going to collapse in a heap with exhaustion.

'Please, enough of that. You're a good mum. What happened to Lexy – it took an experienced doctor and a bit of good luck to pick it. You couldn't have known, Mrs. Popovich.'

'Could you call me Silvia? I'm not used to all this Mrs. Popovich stuff. I wonder who everyone's talking to.'

'Fine. And I'm Brendan.'

'Irish.'

'The name. Me, I'm just an Aussie.'

'You got kids?'

'Not yet. But we'll have a whole cricket team if Molly gets her way.'

'Molly? Oh, of course. At the farm. She's nice. Bit way out.'

'Yeah. That's Moll.'

'Nice place you got too. Sort of place Janni and I always wanted. Somewhere good to bring up kids ...'

'You know what I think, Silvia? Kids don't care what sort of home they've got. So long as it's filled with love. Lexy's got you and his grandfather and that's a hell of a start.'

'You really believe that?' she asked uncertainly.

'You bet I do.'

Lexy stirred again and opened his eyes. 'Mummy?'

Silvia was instantly alert again. 'I'm here, little man. I'm right here.'

Lexy tried to get out of bed but Brendan stepped forward to gently restrain him. 'Well good morning, Lexy! Please, don't get up, we do breakfast in bed in this establishment.'

Confused, Lexy looked at Brendan and then at his mother.

'It's alright, mate. You're in hospital, remember? And you're doing really well.'

'But you need to do what Brendan tells you, darling. Brendan's married to Molly, remember weird Molly?'

Lexy slowly nodded. 'Have the worms gone?'

'All gone,' said Brendan. 'Defeated by Dr Elliott's all-conquering army.'

'Good.'

'Lexy, I have to go to work now. I'll come back to see you later, okay?'

Brendan didn't like the sound of her working. 'Are

you quite sure that's necessary? You've had no sleep.'

'There's a quota to fill. Or we don't get paid.'

Brendan knew how it felt to be short of money. He understood. 'Well at least don't worry about Lexy. We'll be fine here, won't we, mate?' But Lexy had fallen asleep again.

'I'd make my getaway if I were you,' said Brendan, 'but please – do get something to eat? Silvia nodded and thanked him and left. Brendan thought to himself, I bet she picks an apple and calls it breakfast.

Mothers, that's how they were. Martyrdom came with the title. Molly, he knew, would be the same. He grinned to himself. Molly just couldn't wait to try her hand. But for a little while longer, she'd have to practice being a mother to piglets.

Bruce Cameron's feelings about motherhood were somewhat less generous. When he saw Silvia arriving ten minutes late and looking rather the worse for wear he jumped to conclusions. 'This isn't a holiday camp, you know,' was how he greeted her. 'If you want to party all night, that's your business, but there's not much point you turning up here because you're not fit to work.'

'I wasn't partying, Mr. Cameron.'

'Oh, don't give me that. I know what you're like, girlie. All the same, you people. Too much time in the pub, that's your trouble.'

'That's not fair. I spent the night at the hospital, my little boy had an operation!'

Cameron gave her a long, hard look. 'Well, alright. If that's the case, I'm sorry. But I still need you to fill your quota, you can understand that, can't you? Not a charity, love. You and the old man – had my doubts about you from the beginning.'

'I understand. I'll get the work done.'

'Okay then. Hope the kid's better soon.' And he stomped off, having made what he felt was a magnanimous gesture in not having fired her. Silvia watched him go with a mixture of fear and loathing but she got to work picking.

At the clinic, Simon was anxious to talk about his evening with Vicky. Shirley would have much preferred that he didn't.

'She's smart, your daughter. We knew that. But she has a very sharp tongue. She can be quite – well, lacerating is the word that comes to mind. I wonder where she got that from?'

'Simon, right now something is lacerating my brain. Do you think you might have a cure for it?'

'Would it by any chance be due to the third brandy I'm sure I saw you pour last night?'

'That is altogether possible.'

'Mm … there's no miracle that I'm aware of. But let me see.' He disappeared into his surgery and soon returned with a couple of tablets. He put something fizzy in a glass of water and handed it all to her. 'Vitamin B and paracetamol. Tried and true.'

Shirley swallowed the tablets with the Berocca and shuddered at the taste. Simon chattered on. 'Getting back to Vicky, the evening started off really well and then somehow degenerated. One thing, I will *not* be playing polo, I've gone right off that idea. The thought of her constant little digs about it …'

'Oh, I wouldn't stop just because Vicky doesn't approve,' said Shirley. 'I don't think that's likely to impress her.'

'It's not?'

'Well no. I'm sure she'd expect you to stick to your guns. Um, mallet. Whatever. My head is still throbbing.'

'And I'm not helping, right?'

Shirley nodded faintly. Simon sighed. 'I think I might put your daughter in the too-hard basket,' he said and went to make coffee before the first patients arrived. But he hadn't quite finished. 'Frank was a real surprise, wasn't he? Is there anything the man can't do? Cop, chef, horticulturalist. *And* a thoroughly nice bloke, heavens he even washed up! You should really think twice before you let a man like that slip through your fingers, Shirl.'

'You are making the coffee? Or shall I just the call the undertaker?'

Shirley was not the only one feeling out of sorts, Lexy was having a little meltdown of his own. Having suddenly realised that he was all alone in this very strange place called a hospital, he had pulled the blankets up to his chin and was holding them there tightly while letting the tears flow. Brendan, who had come in to give him a wash, was instead using all of his comedic powers to try to calm him down. He started by pretending to examine Lexy's untouched tray.

'So what have we here? Wrong sort of cereal, obviously. Doesn't the kitchen know that five-year-olds only eat weetbix? And wholemeal toast? That's for girls, isn't it? Boys have white toast with peanut butter. No wonder you didn't eat it.'

'Where's my mum?'

'Hey, mate. You know where she is. She's picking apples for Mr. Cameron. She said goodbye. And she said she'd come back the minute she's finished work. Okay?' Lexy gave a faint nod. 'In the meantime, we've got to get on with things. Like having a wash.'

'No! It hurts.'

'If we did the wash thing, we could maybe forget breakfast – just this once – and have dessert instead. Say jelly and ice cream.'

Lexy was beginning to waver. 'It really does hurt.'

'Honestly?' Brendan was giving him the benefit of the

doubt. 'In that case, it might be a job for – Supernurse!' He peeled his white coat back to reveal a Superman T-shirt. Lexy was impressed. He might even have given in except that Terence arrived at that moment.

'Good morning, you have a visitor from Krypton, I see, Lexy.' He turned to Brendan. 'Alright if I examine the patient for a moment?' Poor Brendan, hugely embarrassed, had quickly closed his coat.

'Of course, doctor. He's complaining of some pain.' Brendan moved back.

Terence smiled at Lexy and put a firm hand on the blankets. 'Can I have a look at where we did the operation, Lexy?' The blankets were away before Lexy knew it and Terence was gently prodding the scar. 'Gosh it's looking terrific, you'll need to show your friends before it fades too much. The good thing is that horrible lump has all gone. And in a couple of days, you'll be able to go home. Now where's this pain?'

Lexy waved vaguely in the area of his tummy. 'Well I think I'll hand you back to Supernurse now. And if it gets really bad he can give you a pill. Alright?'

Lexy nodded. Terence said to Brendan, 'I'm not too concerned. But of course he can have paracetamol if he needs it. Up, up and away.' Lexy watched him ago, not quite sure.

'A bit of a scrub up, then?' suggested Brendan brightly.

'Ice cream after?'

'Deal.'

'Okay.'

Not all the residents of Wandin Valley were being so amenable. Doris had not only managed to get out of her sty, she had dug up and totally destroyed the banksia rose which Frank had so recently given Molly and which Molly had planted with great care, hoping it would grow to beautify Doris's quarters. So much for gratitude. Molly was beginning to wonder if mating Doris was a good idea after all or whether looking at her in terms of so much ham and bacon might not a better proposition.

Even more cantankerous than Doris was Artie Turner, who was sitting in his usual spot on the front porch with the racing guide open, marking the horses he'd back if flaming Pat would let him have a bet. The fact that his picks invariably lost, and they'd be church mouse-poor if she *had* let him, did not enter Artie's reasoning. Next door, Emily was doing her best to pick some flowers, roses and salvias. The latter grew close to the fence and it didn't take long for Artie to get nasty.

'Doing a bit of spying through the cracks, are we Emily? Seeing what old Artie's up to today? Well I can give you a tip for the third at Caulfield if that's any help but I don't suppose you're a betting girl, are you, love? Too up yourself to have a flutter on the gee-gees.'

'You really are tiresome, Artie. I adore horses, as you know well. Used to go to the Cup every year without fail. As for spying, if I wanted to know anything about your miserable life, I'd barge right in and ask Patricia. I am *trying* to pick a few flowers.' She did not add that she was expecting a guest that evening.

'So you say, so you say...'

Emily was wickedly thinking how nice it would be to play the bad fairy, to pass the old curmudgeon a rose that would prick his finger and put him to sleep for a hundred years, when Pat came out.

'I hope you're not being a pest, Dad,' she said. Artie denied it but Pat presumed the worst. She also saw that Emily needed help and quickly went next door to help with the flowers. 'Was he being awful?'

'No worse than usual. How are your plans for Somers going?'

'Oh, Emily, it's out of the question, you know it is.'

'Let's wait and see, shall we?' Other people's problems were easily solved for Emily Page. It was her own life that was rapidly becoming impossible.

CHAPTER ELEVEN

Silvia's Popovich's life seemed more impossible than it was. She just needed to stop and take a deep breath and get a new slant on things. Not at this very moment, of course; right now, she was doggedly picking apples, even though the other pickers had all gone to lunch. Halfway through the break, and still wearing her overalls, she dashed off to the hospital. Lexy's eyes did not light up as she expected when she entered his room.

'Hello, darling.'

'Hi.'

From her pocket she took out a little wooden frog. 'See what Grandpa made you. Isn't he beautiful?' And he was indeed carved with great skill.

Lexy took the frog and fingered it but didn't comment. 'Lexy? What's the matter? I saw Matron a minute ago. She said the doctor's very pleased, you're doing well.'

'I'm not, it hurts!'

Silvia was alarmed. 'What? Where does it hurt?'

'My tummy. There's a big pain! It hurts all the time!'

Silvia pressed the call button and then ran to the door, yelling for help. 'Nurse! Somebody!'

It was actually Marta who came, with Terence, who was in the next ward, close behind. Marta calmed Silvia and Terence examined Lexy yet again but as before, could find nothing amiss. He drew Silvia aside.

'I really can't find anything wrong, Mrs. Popovich. The wound's fine, there's no infection. To be honest, I've been here most of the morning and Lexy's been laughing and joking with Brendan, having a great time from the sound of it.'

'Brendan the nurse?'

'Yes. He can be very entertaining. Maybe *too* entertaining.'

'Perhaps Lexy got a little over-excited,' said Marta.

'But this pain …'

'He's had an operation,' Terence said. There's going to be *some* pain. I think Brendan's done a good job of distracting him.'

'So you're absolutely sure he's okay?'

'Look.' Terence moved even further away and dropped his voice. 'There's always a chance – just the tiniest chance – of more cysts forming on Lexy's liver. We can't rule that out altogether. It's highly unlikely but we do need to keep an eye on him. When you move on, I'll give you a letter about it. Down the track, it could mean a further operation.'

'And more and more?'

'It's most unlikely. The best thing you can do, sadly, is encourage Lexy not to play with stray dogs. Certainly don't let them lick him. And always, always, if he does have contact with dogs, he must wash his hands afterwards.'

Silvia nodded. She glanced over at Lexy, she looked tired out, Terence thought. 'You know, I'm more worried about you, Mrs. Popovich. I'd like you to stay here and have a meal, I'm sure we could organise that. And a nice long rest on that spare bed.'

'I can't do that. The lunch break's nearly over, I've got to get back. I'll lose my job if I don't.' She kissed Lexy and told him to be good and was gone before more pressure could be brought to bear.

Terence shook his head. 'She'll be our next patient.' He went over to Lexy. 'Your mummy works too hard. See if you can help her by having a sleep.' Lexy seemed willing enough to obey and slid down under the blankets. Though he really wasn't concerned, Terence told Marta to call him if there was any change at all in the boy's condition.

The long afternoon wore on. There was still plenty of warmth in the sun but once it had gone the chill of autumn settled on the valley and the pickers were glad to leave the orchard. Most were finished by the time the school bus dropped the kids off. Tiffany was amongst them and she stopped to ask Silvia about Lexy before going to join her mum and dad, full of the day's doings. When Silvia saw Tiffany she did wonder if she was right about school but all kids weren't as well-adjusted as Tiffany Brownlow. Alex had knocked off earlier, he'd already done more than usual and his back wouldn't cope any longer but Silvia went on picking apples. She was still picking when Molly next door was locking up her chickens and Bill Ferguson, a few kilometres further down the road, was finishing off the milking.

Bill was not feeling well. He was nauseous, he had a pain in his abdomen, backache: bloody cystitis again. It was supposed to be a woman's disease, women and old blokes, how come he had it anyway? Well it was too late to go to the doctor, it would have to wait till morning. He let the last cow out, turned the machines off, did a minimal clean up and staggered up to the house and made a cup of tea. While he did, and feeling just a little sorry for himself, it struck him that it was times like this he missed having a wife. Not when things were going along on an even keel, but the bad times and the good times – that's when you wanted someone by your side. He turned on the television for the early news. There was a story about President Reagan being wounded by a gunman; another about the recently engaged Prince Charles and Lady Diana Spencer. Bill thought it was just as well young Charlie had found himself a woman at last; God in that job, he'd need one. Bill managed a smile. He reckoned that if he was heir to a kingdom and a rather large fortune he could probably get a sheila himself.

Silvia by now was working on automatic pilot. The apples continued to fall into the basket. She barely noticed that it was almost dark and no one knew she was still in the orchard. The dizziness overcame her so suddenly she didn't have time to climb down the ladder. She blacked out and crashed to the ground and her basket of golden delicious went with her, spilling out and rolling in all directions, here and there catching a last flash of light from the setting sun amongst the dark shadows.

That is where Alex found her, hidden in the dark now, much later. After she failed to come back to the camping ground for dinner, he'd used the public phone at the office to ring the hospital and discovered she wasn't there either. Then he'd panicked and gone to the orchard.

Silvia was barely conscious and Alex didn't want to move her. He banged on the Camerons' door but got no answer so ran on to the Jones's. By the time Brendan answered he was so out of breath he could barely explain what had happened.

***

When Marta rang Terence he'd already made something of a dint in a bottle of Scotch – but not such a dint that he couldn't drive. He got to the hospital moments before Brendan and Alex arrived with Silvia. They examined the patient, took x-rays, cleaned her lacerated arm which seemed – along with a sprained ankle – to have suffered most of the damage. Fortunately, although mildly concussed, she appeared to have avoided any serious head injury.

Terence spent some time checking the x-rays of her arm while she lay on the operating table then gave his opinion that she was in fact lucky, it could have been a great deal worse. Silvia wanted to know if the arm was broken and he quickly reassured her that it wasn't, nor was there any nerve damage. 'We've got quite a bit of fancy stitching to do. But it should be right as rain.'

Silvia sighed with relief. 'Thank goodness. Just so long as I can get back to work.'

'Well. Maybe in three weeks or so.'

Silvia became agitated. She couldn't wait three weeks, didn't they understand? She had to work tomorrow or she and her father-in-law would both lose their jobs. If they'd bandage the arm it would be okay …

With that she struggled to sit up and nearly fainted with the pain. Brendan gently eased her back flat. 'Please, Silvia. I know it's asking the impossible. But this one time, you've got to lie there and let other people take care of you.' And scared and worried as she was, she trusted him enough to do as he asked.

There had been no need, as things tuned out, to call Simon to the hospital so his evening of mahjong with Emily Page had not been interrupted. Unlike Silvia, he was enjoying himself immensely and had in fact begun to do so over their first sherry. (Vicky had been right about the sherry.)

'I had an interesting telephone conversation yesterday, Emily,' Simon began.

'Did you, dear? With whom?'

'An old friend of yours. He mentioned Alexandria. Such an exciting place, he said, during the war. Such an uncommonly interesting mix of people. And as for the girls ... like a bunch of spring flowers, he said.'

'Really? How uncommonly poetic.'

'Of course everyone was in transit, wasn't that so? Shipping in and out, on leave, some of them wounded, getting patched up so they could fight again.'

'True.'

'A lot of those spring flowers must have been nurses, I guess, doing the patching up. You were one of them, Emily, weren't you?'

'What if I was?'

'That's how you got to know Grandie. He told me. He was an army surgeon.'

'I neither confirm nor deny anything.'

Simon dropped his bantering tone a little. 'Such times they must have been. Exciting and heartbreaking. What happened? Did he overstep the mark? Were you shipped off somewhere else?'

'I think it's time we played the first round,' said Emily Page. Simon got his own back by winning with ease. Emily was gracious in defeat.

'Quite a change for me, I always beat Harriet. I do miss Harriet.'

Simon asked about her family; did they ever come to visit?

'Oh, they do, but they're scattered all over the place. Sydney, Adelaide ... we try to get together at Christmas. I'd love to see more of my grandchildren but they lead such busy lives. You must remember what it was like being a teenager. And one doesn't want to be a burden. Be a dear and make another pot of coffee.' Simon made the coffee and wondered why families always left it until it was too late.

Vicky Dean was trying to be gracious but it was an uphill battle. It was now two o'clock in the morning and she was on the phone to the redoubtable Beverley who ran the local telephone exchange. Beverley, who sounded so bright it was indecent, apparently had no need of sleep. There was, it seemed, a cow at Jacob's place in need of veterinary assistance. Vicky shouldn't have queried why Colin Jacobs had asked for her. It did nothing for her spirits to discover that the other vet had refused the call-out 'unless Bev couldn't find anyone else.' Vicky found the excuse he'd given – a bad hangover – utterly pathetic. But thinking of the money, and the labouring heifer, she agreed to go.

'It'll take me a good half-hour, Bev. But tell him I'll be there as fast as I can.' Stifling a yawn she hung up and started pulling overalls on, on top of her pyjamas. Shirley staggered out from the bedroom.

'Two a.m.? Can't it wait?'

Vicky shook her head. 'It's Colin Jacobs' prize Jersey heifer, she's having a difficult labour.' Vicky grinned. 'Bev says she got freaked out by some of the pickers.'

'Bev did? Or the heifer?'

'I'm not sure. But the Jacobs don't have fruit trees.'

Shirley had disappeared back into her bedroom. 'I wonder who'll get blamed for every minor disaster when the pickers leave town?'

'Yeah, they'll be missed, won't they? Well, I'm off.'

'Hang on, I'm coming with you.'

'Mum! No. As you said, it's two a.m.!'

'That's why. There's a prowler around. You shouldn't be out and about by yourself.'

'I'm sure if you rang Sergeant Gilroy he'd offer to escort me.'

'And I'm sure two women can handle the situation. Shall we go?'

'*I'll* go. You go back to bed. Truly, I'll be fine. Look, it's a heifer. If it's a big calf, I could be hours, you mightn't even get to work on time.'

Shirley could see the sense in that and reluctantly gave in. 'Be careful, alright? If anyone tries to flag you down, run them over.'

'Mum, of course. I'll just flatten them.' She gave Shirley a hug and left her there to worry.

'And turn the radio on!' Shirley called after her. 'So you don't fall asleep!'

Alex Popovich had long ago succumbed to sleep on a bench in the hospital corridor. Silvia had been sedated, expertly stitched up and put to bed but he had not wanted to leave his family and go home alone. He blamed himself for their current predicament. He should have tried harder to find permanent work after Janni died. He forgot that he had tried for months to no avail, that few bosses were prepared to look beyond the picture he presented of an ageing immigrant with imperfect English.

Marta found him there on the bench as she was about to go home and read much of his struggle in his sleeping face and felt more than a little empathy. To create a new life in a new land was not an undertaking for the faint-hearted as she herself knew well. She got a blanket and a pillow and tried to make Alex more comfortable but he woke up. He began to apologise but she stopped him.

'Please, it is quite alright. But you'd be better at home, Mr. Popovich. Getting some real rest. They are going to need you.'

'I am afraid that Silvia will try to leave. To go back to work.'

'I promise you, we will not allow that to happen.'

'Will you tell her … ask Brendan to tell her … she must not worry about the picking. It is not much of a job anyway, we will manage somehow. Nothing matters so much as her health.'

'We'll make sure she understands.' Marta smiled. 'We will tie her to the bed if necessary.'

Alex got up then and thanked her and bid her goodnight and slowly made his way to the door. Marta herself had a last word to the night nurse in charge then went to collect her bag and her car-keys. That was as far as she got.

Marta's office, normally a room with a place for everything and everything in its place, had been ransacked. Furniture had been overturned, filing cabinets had been opened and papers were strewn across the floor. The one thing the intruder had not gained access to was the drug room, which had an unobtrusive door off Marta's office and which was still locked. Whether that was down to a want of effort or a lack of interest, Frank Gilroy would have to work out in due course.

CHAPTER TWELVE

Marta had done a careful inventory by the time Frank
arrived and, like Molly before her, could find nothing
missing.

'What do you think he was after?' she asked Frank,
then hastened to add, 'he or she.'

'It's a he if it's the same person who went to the
Jones' place. I don't know, Matron. It's usually drugs or
money.' He had a good look around. 'He's made a mess
alright. But he hasn't done a lot of damage. So I doubt if
he's the violent type.'

'Perhaps he was interrupted. Alex Popovich came out
to the corridor to rest on the bench. His daughter-in-law
and grandson are both patients here.'

Frank nodded. 'I'll follow that up in the morning,
then.'

'He'll be here or at Cameron's.' Marta sighed. 'Do
you think perhaps it's one of the pickers?'

Frank shrugged. 'They'll get blamed either way,
Matron, won't they?' There wasn't much more Frank
could do at that hour. He left to file his report and Marta

got one of the night staff to help her clean up before going home to sleep through what was left of the night.

Alex had gone back to the camping ground, parked the wagon and walked to the toilet block. On his way back he found that he was not the only one about at this late hour. The young man who a few days before had almost knocked Silvia flying, mumbled something in reply to Alex's greeting, veered off the track and disappeared into his small tent. Like several others in Wandin Valley, he too was in pain but could find nothing at all to relieve it.

The day of Doris's nuptials broke damp and dismal. It could have been taken, had Molly believed in omens, as a sign of things to come. Fortunately it was still dark when she woke to the sound of Brendan banging around in the kitchen and she could not see the extent of the storm clouds louring over the valley.

Terence Elliott, inspecting his grapes with Ian Jamieson sometime later, could see it only too well.

'What happens if that hits us?' he asked, waving towards the heavens.

Ian grinned. 'If you're going to farm, Terence, you have to learn there's not a damn thing you can do about the weather. Accept it as part of the deal or you'll go crazy. That storm could do a lot of damage or it might pass you by.'

'Right.'

'Wait till you've been here ten years.'

'It gets easier?'

Ian shook his head. 'Not if hail wipes out your whole vintage. That never gets easy.'

'I'm an optimist,' Terence said. 'When do you think the grapes'll be ready?'

'Another week. Maybe two. Patience.'

***

Marta, showing infinite patience in spite of having had very little sleep, was explaining to Lexy that his mum had hurt her arm and was now also in the hospital.

'How did she get here?'

'Well your grandpa got Brendan to help him and they brought her in together.'

Lexy turned to his hero who was also present. 'Thanks,' he said.

'My pleasure,' said Brendan.

'Where's grandpa now?'

'I sent him home to have some sleep,' said Marta.

Lexy nodded. 'Can I see Mum?'

'Maybe Brendan could take you. Just for a minute.' So with Lexy ensconced in a wheelchair they went visiting and found Silvia two doors down sound asleep.

'Mummy's tired.'

'Mummies often get tired.'

'She's *always* tired,' Lexy said sadly. 'Grandpa says she works too hard.'

'Well she's having a good rest today,' Brendan said brightly. 'Shall we go and explore a little bit while we've got this nice wheelchair?'

Driving home from the Jacobs' place, Vicky Dean was fighting to stay awake. Part of it was sheer exhaustion; part of it was a desire to wipe the whole horrible night from her mind. In spite of her best efforts, the valuable calf had not survived, though she had saved its mother. Colin Jacobs, doing his best to help her, had not laid any blame, had in fact thanked her generously for her efforts. But Vicky still wondered, over and over again, what else she could have done, or done better. In truth there was nothing; the labour had been protracted, the little heifer was worn out and the calf was far too big, a blueprint for disaster. All the same, Vicky felt a failure.

Lost in these thoughts, she almost didn't stop when she saw Bill Ferguson's car leaving his farm. Or rather – which was the odd thing – not leaving. It was stopped in the middle of the open gateway. The car door was open. But there was no sign anywhere of Bill. Vicky parked on the edge of the road and walked towards the gate. She got closer and then broke into a run because she could see Bill slumped over the steering wheel.

At the clinic, Shirley was opening a parcel and telling Simon how Vicky still wasn't home when she left the house.

'We should have chosen our careers more carefully. School-teaching. Something with sensible hours.'

'You don't know many schoolteachers, do you?' said Shirley. 'Exam time, marking, weekend sport, camps …'

'Banking, then.' He peered at the book Shirley had unwrapped. 'Larousse?'

Shirley gave him a look. 'It's about Tai Chi. Some of us care more for the mind than the body.'

'Fair enough. And I'm sure Frank'll whip you up a yummy barbecued pork to have when you've finished being spiritual.'

Bev rang before Shirley could use the book, which was large and heavy, in a well-aimed assault. Vicky had found Bill Ferguson collapsed in his car and couldn't move him on her own. She needed the ambulance or at least a strong male.

Shirley told Simon that Terence had sent the ambulance to get Miss Bird just half an hour ago, her lupus had flared again and she wasn't coping.

'Then I'll go, Vicky and I can manage between us. Ring the hospital, Shirl? And reshuffle any appointments?' He grabbed his bag and dashed out as his first patient came in the door: Yvette Sampson, aged seventeen. He thought that he owed Bill Ferguson a beer.

***

Marta was quietly tearing her hair out. Wandin Valley Bush Nursing Hospital, as she was pointedly telling Brendan, was not Royal North Shore. There was a limit to the number of beds. There was a limit even to the beds at Burrigan Hospital. And both were currently, officially, full. If this were the city they would be sending patients elsewhere. But it was the country; there was no 'elsewhere'.

'What have you done with Birdie?' she asked Brendan.

'Put her in with poor Silvia. I'll make sure Silvia gets some earplugs. Or she can just pretend to be deaf. It was that or have her share with Lexy. Hey, maybe we should do that …'

'What are you thinking?'

'Oh … maybe let Bill Ferguson share with Silvia?'

'A little bit of matchmaking, Mr Jones?'

'Be good for both of them, isn't Bill divorced? And a dairy-farmer, for heaven's sake, how does he manage?'

Marta laughed. 'With difficulty, I'm sure. 'But I think for the sake of decorum, we'd better put Mr Ferguson with Lexy. How is he, by the way? Lexy?'

'Good. The pain seems to have disappeared.'

'Was it ever there, do you think?'

'I think maybe he was enjoying the attention. Not too much at home, you know? Plenty of love, not enough time.'

'Easy to understand,' said Marta. 'Only so many hours, I imagine Silvia never gets a break. Lexy needs a dad as well.'

Brendan grinned. 'Which I think I might just try to arrange.'

Bill Ferguson had roused sufficiently to fight against the very idea of hospital, pointing out that he had eighty cows to milk. He just needed to see Doc Elliott. Simon said he could see Doc Elliott once he was admitted and Vicky said she'd get Hal Secombe to help her organise a roster for the milking. By then Bill had passed out again so that was pretty much the end of the argument. He came to in hospital when Brendan helped him into bed and then Terence came to see him.

'Don't say it, doc. I feel like a prize idiot.'

'So you should. What did I say about the Mandelate capsules?'

'Not to stop taking them.'

'But you felt a bit better so you did.' Bill just nodded. 'And now you're going to be stuck in here for two or three days while we get you sorted out. It's not a joke, this cystitis, Bill. It can lead to very serious kidney disease if it's not treated properly. And that, as I've explained to you, is the last thing you want.'

'I know, doc. I'm sorry.'

'Okay. Now I'm going to get Nurse Jones to put a catheter in so can see what's really going on with your urine. And then he'll introduce you to your room-mate.'

'A *catheter*?' Bill was not impressed but he didn't get much sympathy.

'That's what happens when you don't take your medicine, mate.'

Terence left them to it and Brendan got down to business, chatting away to distract Bill from the procedure. 'We're a bit pushed for space at the moment. So you're sharing with a young man named Lexy Popovich. Great little kid.'

'I know Lexy.'

Brendan was surprised. 'You do?'

'Yeah …' Bill called out through the curtains. 'Hey, Lexy? It's Bill, remember? I helped get your car started?'

'G'day, Bill! What happened to you?' Lexy sounded

pleased to have another friend. Brendan was secretly delighted. He felt with Lexy and Bill knowing each other, his match-making effort was off to a flying start.

Out at the Jones farm, Jerry Percival, a large and gormless teenager, was introducing himself to Molly. By his side, a ring through its nose, was a large boar.

'G'day,' said Jerry. 'You the lady of the house?'

'I'm Molly,' said Molly.

Jerry looked at her coolly: the bejewelled gumboots, the polka-dot skivvy, the overalls covered in pink crocodiles. 'Okay. This here's Landrace Huntington the Third. Come to do your Doris a favour.' He did not tell Molly that Huntington was on a last chance to perform or he'd be turned into salami.

'I was expecting your father. I'm new to this pig-mating business, I might need some help.'

Jerry was not surprised. Looked like she'd stepped off the last bus from the city. 'No worries,' he said. 'Nothin' to it. Just put old Huntington in with your girl and let 'em get on with it.'

'You're sure?'

'Lady, I was born and bred with pigs.'

So the pigs were introduced as well. They grunted a bit. Molly and Jerry left the sty and shut the gate.

'What now?' asked Molly.

'I reckon you make us both a nice cuppa,' said Jerry, 'while we wait developments.'

'You're quite sure Huntington knows what to do?'

'God yes. Been at it for years. Piglets all over the place.' Molly went and made the tea. When she returned, Jerry was sitting on a block of redgum by the woodheap, smoking. She passed him a mug.

'Like your gear,' said Jerry, the fashion expert. 'Get it in the city, do you?'

'I make most of it.'

'Go on. I bet my mum'd like it too. Sort of way out like you, she is.'

Molly doubted it but hated the thought of missing an opportunity. 'I do some dressmaking,' she said. 'If your mum ever wants something. Has there been any sign of activity?'

'Bit quiet, come to think of it.'

The two of them strolled over to the sty and peered in. Doris lay on her side, sound asleep. Huntington the Third lay with his back to her, sound asleep also.

'You didn't hear anything?' Molly said. Jerry shook his head. 'So you wouldn't think it was post-coital exhaustion?' Another shake of the head. 'Experienced, you said. So how exactly does he do it? Father all those piglets?'

Jerry was mortified. 'I'll take him straight to the knackers,' he said. 'Dad won't want him back if he can't perform. No room for bludgers at our place.'

Molly thought that sounded a bit drastic. 'No, hang on. After all, there's no rush. And everyone deserves a second chance, don't you think? You finish your tea, I might just give the vet a ring.'

The vet's advice was to leave the pair alone for a time. Let them get used to each other and see if an interest developed. Molly was not much comforted but the thought of poor, rejected Doris did at least give Vicky something to smile about. She was smiling when Simon walked into her surgery with two takeaway coffees from the only decent café in town.

'I thought you could use this,' he said.

'I could indeed, thanks.' Vicky took the coffee and refrained from commenting on ulterior motives.

'We didn't have much chance to talk before but I gather you had a pretty grim night.'

'Not the best.'

'And yet you're smiling.'

'Molly rang. She has two pigs refusing to mate.'

'You mean Doris has rejected her suitor? Females are so fussy.'

'The other way round, I think. How was your night, no mercy dash to save a dying soul?'

'I played mahjong with Emily, as you well know.'

'And did you drink sherry?'

Simon was annoyed. 'Emily drinks sherry. I was her guest and I joined her. Have the culture police declared it a crime now, sherry-drinking?'

Vicky shrugged. 'You never used to drink it.'

'Not in Wandin Valley, perhaps. Why do you object to my seeing Emily?'

'I don't object, Simon, good heavens, it's none of my business! I just find it a bit odd. She's old enough to be your grandmother.'

'She's also smart and funny and very entertaining. And if I can help to take her mind off things in return – provide her with a bit of pain relief – then we're doing each other a favour. There's no sugar in the coffee. Maybe there should be.'

He left, he was hurt and a little bit angry. He'd gone to console her about the calf, nothing else, to offer a shoulder to cry on if she wanted one. Why did she have to be like that?

Vicky was asking herself the same thing. She put it down to sleep deprivation.

CHAPTER THIRTEEN

Molly had also rung Brendan about Doris's ill-fated coupling and had been hurt by what she perceived to be his lack of interest. She did not perhaps understand exactly how busy they were at the hospital and she took his idea of getting a relationship between Bill and Sylvia off the ground just a little too seriously.

'I don't think it's wise to interfere in other people's love lives, Brendan.'

'I'm planning on being an introduction service, that's all. Like you were with Doris and Landrace Huntingdon III.'

'Yes and look where that's got me!'

'There might still be a happy outcome, Moll.'

She felt he was being facetious. 'And pigs might fly, Brendan!' She hung up.

Jerry had long ago gone home to help his dad so Molly decided to do some sewing, since the window of the sunroom where she worked gave her a good view of the pig pen. She had barely completed two seams before the power went off. Wondering not for the first time what had possessed her to leave the comforts of life in Adelaide, she headed for the shed, pausing on the way to peer discreetly at the lovers. There was so sign whatsoever of amorous activity. Doris was in one corner staring balefully at Huntington who stood with his back to her, snuffling at a bit of hay.

'She's a very nice sow, Huntington,' Molly said. 'Very well-bred. What's the matter with you? Do you bat for the other team or something?'

In the shed she checked the generator for fuel, of which it had plenty, then attacked it even more viciously than usual. 'I don't understand why we have to hurt each other like this!' she yelled, applying a powerful kick as Bob Hatfield had taught her. It was then, as the generator roared into life, that she saw a startled Alex Popovich leap to his feet in the corner of the shed. He gave her quite a fright.

'Oh!' She quickly realised who it was. 'Oh, Mr. Popovich, it's you. Thank goodness. I thought for a moment it was that intruder come back. What on earth are you doing here?'

'I'm afraid I was sleeping. I am sorry. I had nowhere to go.'

'But aren't you staying at the camping ground? Brendan said …'

Alex was shaking his head. 'Not any more.' He was trying very hard, Molly could see, not to break down, not to lose what remained of his dignity. She tried to help.

'I was talking to Brendan a while ago. He happened to mention Silvia. She's alright, Mr Popovich.'

'But she cannot work. And I, on my own …' He shook his head.

'Has that bastard Cameron fired you?'

'Yes. So I cannot afford the camping ground. Please … if I did some jobs for you and your husband, could I stay a few days in one of your sheds? I could cut wood. Or mend things, I am a good carpenter. Just while they are in hospital. Silvia and Lexy.'

Molly thought the sheds were all freezing at night and no place at all for an old man. 'Let's go and have some coffee,' she said. 'I bet you're a coffee person. We'll work out something. I don't suppose you know anything about pigs, do you?'

As Molly had said, physically Silvia was doing fine. Terence had just examined her and was pleased with progress. The long laceration on her arm was healing as expected and all her obs were stable. She was still very run down but a few days in hospital with rest and good food would take care of that. It was her mental state that was troubling both Terence and Marta. She was crying and seemed unable to stop.

'Mrs Popovich … Silvia,' Terence said. 'If you could tell us what's worrying you, then maybe we could help.' She said nothing. 'I hope it's not Lexy, he's really fine. Matron tells me the pain's all gone. We think it was too much ice-cream.'

'And maybe also he liked to be the centre of attention for a change. He didn't want to go home too soon.'

'It's not Lexy,' said Silvia through the tears.

'Then …?' Terence asked gently and when she didn't respond, 'You know what they say about a problem shared?'

Finally it all spilled out. Silvia was sure she would have lost her job, probably Alex had too, he couldn't fill their quota without her and Cameron had threatened them enough. Now they would have no money. She didn't know what they would do.

Terence pointed out that for the moment she and Lexy were both being fed and cared for. 'That's the whole thing, doctor! It's this place. The hospital. How am I going to pay for this? And you?'

Terence was stumped. He thought he could waive his bill easily enough but he could hardly speak for the hospital board and the health department. It was Marta who came to the rescue.

'Surely you're a member of the Union, Silvia?'

'Yes.'

'Well the accident happened on the job. You'll be covered by Workers' Compensation.'

'See? A problem shared and you've got a solution. Now please. Try to get some rest.'

Silvia was profuse with her thanks. As Terence and Marta were leaving, a voice from the next bed said, 'What does a body have to do to get a cup of tea around here?'

'Soon, Birdie, soon,' said Marta.

'Silvia, is it?' said the indefatigable Birdie.

'That's right.'

'I'm Norah. But everyone calls me Birdie. I used to do a bit of droving in my younger days. Out along the Castlereagh. Now that's the life, let me tell you …'

'Perhaps,' whispered Marta to Terence, 'Birdie will lull Silvia to sleep.'

Molly had made coffee for Alex, come to a loose arrangement with him about the spare room off the verandah and – because she knew it would help to repair his tattered self-esteem – had given him some work in her vegetable patch. One look at her efforts there and he would see, she was sure, that it was no act of charity. She'd been back at her sewing for half an hour when Frank Gilroy arrived. He was off-duty, he'd come to get some chicken litter for his roses. But a country cop is never off duty.

'You've got someone working for you now?' he said, while Molly filled the kettle.

'Oh, that's Alex. He lost his job and I need a hand with the veggie garden … he's staying for a day or two while the rest of the family's in hospital.'

'Not Alex Popovich?' said Frank.

'Yes, why?'

Frank explained that he'd been looking for Alex, there was a faint hope he might have some information about the intruder. Molly did know he was at the hospital last night? Molly nodded. She was peering out the window. 'Something up?'

'Just the pigs, Frank. As a farmer I feel like a total failure.' She explained in great detail – far too much detail for Frank's liking – how they were refusing to mate. She told him how Doris was most definitely in season, it was easy to tell. She was restless, twitching her tail, peeing all time, her vulva was quite swollen – it was at that point that Frank interrupted.

'Look, I really don't know a thing about pigs.'

'Well it seems that I don't either. I did everything the book said – everything! – and the Percivals' boar is just totally ignoring her!'

He could see how upset she was and he felt for her. 'Look. Molly. I'm sure these things happen to everyone. Every pig. Pig-farmer. Give it time.'

'That's what Vicky said.'

'See? She'd know. Why don't you make the tea while I have a quick word with Alex?'

But Shirley arrived before he could get out the door. 'Shirl? What are you doing here?'

Shirley asked the same question at the same time and got in first with an answer. 'Molly's making me a tai chi outfit. You?'

'Oh, I came to get some chicken litter for my roses. Going to have a word with Alex Popovich while I'm here about the break in at the hospital.'

'I'm sure Alex didn't do it!'

'No, Shirl, but he was there. Might have seen something.'

'Oh. I suppose that's possible.' She turned to Molly. 'Vicky says the pigs aren't performing.'

'No, they're not,' Molly agreed sadly.

'Maybe we can help.'

Frank looked appalled at this suggestion. Molly was a little bemused. 'You know about pigs, Shirley?'

'Not a lot, but I had a peep on the way in. He's a great lump, that boar, isn't he?' Maybe if the three of us gave him a bit of a lift up, you know?'

Frank decided he was terribly pushed for time and might leave the litter for now. Besides, the storm that had been building up all day seemed likely to break at any minute. He dashed off to have a word to Alex.

'Not like you to desert the field, Frank!' Shirley called after him.

'You know something?' Molly said. 'I'm not sure I want Doris's piglets sired by a lazy sod like Huntington the Third anyway. Let's forget it, shall we? Show me the pattern for this tunic.'

'It's fairly simple. If you're happy to do it I could get the fabric tomorrow.'

Brendan had no intention of abandoning his role as a marriage broker. As he took dinner trays around to Bill and Lexy he thought what fun it would be if it actually worked out. He did not expect that it would, too much of the fairytale in that ending, but it amused him to think about it. He was not used to taking dinner trays to patients – nor to doing many of the tasks which befell him in this small hospital when they were short-staffed – but he did not mind in the least; these rather mundane duties often brought him closer to those he was caring for, made the relationship between nurse and patient more informal. Brendan liked that, he was by nature gregarious and easy-going.

Twice the corridor was lit up by lightning, then as Brendan entered the room an enormous crack of thunder almost made him drop the trays.

'Wow, that was a loud one.'

'Can you open the curtains so we can see, Brendan? Bill and I like storms.'

'Righto. I rather like them myself.' He put the trays down and slowly pulled the curtains right back. He did not notice the sudden movement on the other side. It might have been a person stepping quickly away; perhaps it was just a dancing shadow from one of the trees as the wind increased. The rain started slowly at first, big, fat drops, followed by more lightning, more thunder and then the heavens opened.

'Wouldn't be surprised if it turned to hail,' Bill said. 'Pity the poor fruit-growers if it does.'

'Not Mr Cameron,' said Lexy. 'He's horrible. I don't care what happens to his apples.'

'Out of the mouths of babes,' murmured Bill to Brendan.

'Bill's got lots of cows, Brendan,' Lexy said. 'And I told him you've got a pig.'

'A pig called – what's her name again?'

'Doris. Molly's been trying to get her mated. Not much luck.'

'What's mated?' Lexy wanted to know.

'You're the farmer, mate,' Brendan said to Bill and left him to it as the rain did indeed turn to hail.

'They've got flash-flooding at Widgeera,' Shirley was saying to Vicky, 'I heard it on the radio. Why do we always get storms when crops are ready to harvest?'

'Because farming's hell,' Vicky said. 'Almost as bad as being a vet.' She was drying her hair, having got drenched on a mad dash between a client's house and her car.

'I got home just in time,' Shirley said, 'I went out to see Molly Jones. She's making me an outfit for tai chi.'

'Tai chi? This is the latest fad, is it? Martial arts?'

'It is not just martial arts. It is all about health and spirituality.'

'I see. So no more pyramid?'

'The two are perfectly compatible. How's Simon, by the way?'

'What?' It seemed like a non sequitur for a moment. 'Oh. I see. I do love the way your mind works. He brought me coffee this morning. Very devious.'

'Or perhaps he was just being kind. After all, he knows what it's like to sit up all night with a patient, only to lose them. We're just having chops for dinner, is that all right?' Shirley disappeared into the kitchen.

'Yes, of course. Fine.' But Vicky was thinking of what she had just said. Sometimes her mother could be horribly perspicacious. Vicky hated that.

Some time later, with the storm still raging, Brendan was passing Marta's office when he saw a figure behind the glass, one that was most definitely not the matron. As he went in a young man in jeans and a hooded top collapsed on the floor in front of him.

'What's the matter? Are you ill?'

'It's the pain, doc. It's something awful. You got to help me.'

'What's your name?'

'Michael Harris. Please. I can't stand it.'

'Okay, Michael. I'm a nurse, not a doctor. I'm going to call someone to assist me. Hang on there.'

Simon Bowen, who was on call, got to the hospital as quickly as he could through the tail end of the storm. Hailstones were piled up by the side of the road. He kept wondering if anything were left of Terence's beautiful grapes. By the time he arrived, Brendan and Marta had Michael on a trolley in the examination cubicle. Marta took Simon aside.

'It's all a bit odd, Simon. Brendan found him in my office. He claims to have a kidney stone and he does seem to be in a lot of pain. He's certainly unwell.'

'But you're not sure?'

'Exactly.'

Simon introduced himself to Michael and conducted an examination, initially taking the patient at his word. Apart from proclaiming now and then that he was about to die, and demanding pain killers, Michael was a little calmer.

Afterwards, Simon discussed the case with Marta. All the symptoms for renal colic were there; Michael showed abdominal guarding and rigidity without rebound tenderness so appendicitis was unlikely.

'So you are thinking …?' said Marta.

'Well obviously we need to do more tests, an I.V.P. in particular, so he'll need to go to Burrigan first thing in the morning.'

'But tonight?'

Simon was in a quandary. Marta was puzzled by his indecision but something was nagging at him. 'It's tricky, abdominal pain. Treating it before we really know what's wrong …'

'But you said yourself – he's got all the symptoms of renal colic.'

'I'm not sure he isn't faking it, Marta.'

Marta was stunned. 'Really? You mean he's – what? A drug addict?'

'There was the break in the other night. Then Brendan finds this guy in your office. Most patients don't walk into your office.' Marta acknowledged that. 'And I've seen it before, in emergency. Over and over. Academy Award winning performances, exactly like this chap. So some first year resident gives them a shot of pethidine and hallelujah, the junkie leaves with a smile on his face, praising the lord.'

'This boy, Michael – the pain seems very real.'

'Like I said, amazing actors.'

'So what do you want to do?'

Simon took a deep breath. 'Give him a placebo, Marta. Ten ml of sterile water, it can't do any harm, and with luck, if he *thinks* it's pethidine, it might keep him calm.'

Michael was pleased to get the injection; less so with the idea of going to Burrigan. He was a picker, he said, and couldn't afford to miss work.

Simon pointed out that another attack like the one that brought him here could end the season for him; surely he wanted to find out what was really going on and get proper treatment?

Michael seemed to see the wisdom of that. 'I guess,' he said. 'Alright. Que sera.'

Marta couldn't help a little smile. Simon's junkie was a philosopher now?

Molly was trying very hard to be philosophical about her lost hopes for a sty full of fat pink piglets in the not too distant future. 'We've left them together overnight,' she said. 'For all the good it'll do.'

'Well the storm's gone,' said Brendan. 'There's a dear little sickle moon. Lots of twinkly stars …' Molly gave him a look which suggested it might be wise not to continue. 'All I meant,' said Brendan, sipping his beer, 'was that while there's life there's hope.'

'I don't think Huntington the Third can look forward to much more life,' said Molly darkly. 'Gary Percival rang and talked about salami a lot. How's your match-making going?'

'Good, good.'

'I'm happy for you,' Molly said. 'But I wouldn't mention it to Alex. I'd hate to get his hopes up.'

'Where is he now?'

'Lying down. His back's really hurting him. You didn't mind that I let him stay here?'

'Good heaven's no. I'm glad there's someone here. With all the weirdos round the place. Or maybe it's just one weirdo.' He filled her in on their strange patient.

'It might not be the same person.'

'Probably isn't,' Brendan agreed. 'But I still think we should get a dog. Or two.'

Molly ignored that. 'Hey, doesn't Lexy think *I'm* a weirdo?'

'Not any more. Now you're plain old Molly. Wife of Supernurse.' He put an arm around her and kissed her neck and murmured, 'Shall I give you a demonstration of my totally awesome powers?'

'Do you know what I'd really love?' Molly murmured back. 'If you went and gave a few clues to Huntington the Third.'

CHAPTER FOURTEEN

Marta was feeling in need of some supernatural powers. She was exhausted from doing too many shifts but could see no end to it until Judy Loveday returned from holidays. Agency nurses were hard to come by in country towns. She was doing her rounds now and was thankful to find the hospital peacefully sleeping. Even Miss Bird was off in dreamland, no doubt moving a mob of cattle along the outer Barcoo. But when Marta got to Michael Harris's room, the bed was empty.

She found him in her office; searching wildly, erratically for what could only be drugs. 'Mr Harris! What on earth are you doing?'

'Just stay where you are. You think I don't know what you did, you and that doctor? It wasn't peth you gave me, was it? Nothing for the pain! Well I'll help myself!'

'I can't let you do that. You're endangering your health.'

'You just try to stop me!'

'Matron,' said a little voice. 'Can I have a drink of water? I pressed the buzzer over and over but no-one came.' Marta looked down and saw Lexy standing beside her. 'Who's that man?'

Michael took a couple of steps towards him. Marta quickly put herself between them. 'Don't even think about it,' she said.

'Then give me the drugs.'

'They're kept in the drug room.'

'So where's that?'

The conversation she'd so recently had with Brendan, about guns and what she'd do in a situation like this one, flashed through Marta's mind. She felt in her pocket for her keys and tossed them to Michael. 'It's the locked door there. And the locked grey cupboard inside. The gold key. Take what you want and get out of here.'

It didn't take long. Michael stuffed his pockets with God knew what drugs. They spilled everywhere, out of the cupboard, over the floor. He left without a word. Marta was shaking. Lexy was puzzled as children are by what they cannot quite fathom.

'Was that man being naughty, Matron?'

'Very naughty, Lexy. Now let's get that water and get you back to bed.'

Wandin Valley woke next morning to a pale sun in a washed blue sky. It revealed a trail of destruction which was totally random and which proved that goodness and justice did not always go hand in hand; the hail missed the Eldershaw Estate completely but it also missed Bruce Cameron's orchard. Others were not so fortunate. Ian Jamieson, for instance, was glad he'd agreed to take Terence Elliot's cabernet because most of his own was ruined. People cursed or thanked their lucky stars and got on with the clean up.

Frank Gilroy visited Marta Kurtesz yet again and took more details; at least they now had a name and a full description of their intruder. That he was a drug addict seemed highly probable.

Terence arrived at the clinic to find a pensive Shirley nursing a cup of tea. 'You've been to the hospital?'

Terence nodded. 'Marta was still there. I don't think she's had any sleep.'

'Quite a night,' Shirley said. 'And not just the storm. Bill Ferguson, the Popoviches – did you know that Cameron fired the old man? Just like Bruce to put the boot in when someone's down.'

'I hadn't caught up with that.'

'Molly's got him staying out there for now … that's odd.' She was peering into the dregs in her teacup.

'What is?'

'The tea leaves … there's a man and a small boy in there. Surrounded by grapevines. Looks like your vineyard, Terence.' She looked at him innocently. 'I heard the hail missed you, but there must be work to do out there all the same.'

'I don't believe in tea leaves, Shirl, you know that. Is Simon in yet?'

Shirley didn't push her little vision. She nodded towards the closed door of Simon's surgery. 'Just a little bit fragile? I'll make you both some coffee.'

Terence found a mortified Simon wringing his hands over the bad call he'd made the night before.

'When I think what could have happened, Terence! He could have attacked Marta, taken the little boy hostage …'

'But he didn't.'

'What if he had?'

'Simon, please. Stop it now. You made a risky but not unreasonable decision in the circumstances, based on your experience. The wrong treatment could have been catastrophic, we all know that.'

'I should have given him the pethidine.'

'Yes – with hindsight. Marvellous thing, twenty-

twenty hindsight.' Simon did not appear consoled. 'You've got to let it go, mate. Nothing bad happened. Well, not to anyone else. Harris appears to be a junkie. As such, he's got no one but himself to blame.'

'I hope Frank finds him quickly,' Simon said. 'He just about emptied the drug cupboard, apparently. He could very easily kill himself with that lot.'

'If he's on heroin he's killing himself anyway,' Terence said. His tone surprised Simon; there was a degree of anger that was unexpected. Terence finished his coffee; his tone lightened. 'I'm going to visit Emily this morning. Don't worry, she's your patient now. But Artie Turner's mine.'

Simon actually managed a smile. 'And you and the redoubtable Emily will devise a plan to save Pat.'

'Emily seems to think it's possible. *I* think it will take a miracle.'

No miracle had occurred at the Jones' farm overnight. No Eros or Aphrodite had visited the pig pen and stoked the fires of porcine affection. It was still a Mexican standoff between Doris and Huntington the Third.

'What do you think, Alex?' asked Molly, as they inspected the pair together. 'What would you do where you come from?'

'The same in Serbia as here, Molly. That boar is a big, fat, useless tub of lard. He makes excellent sausages.'

Molly rang Gary Percival and some time later a humiliated Huntington made his exit. Molly did her best to console her girl. 'You did your best, Doris. There's no pleasing some pigs. We'll find you another boar. A less boorish boar. Someone altogether more suitable. Don't you worry about it.' Doris did not, in fact, seem all that concerned. Yes, she was ready to mate but perhaps Huntington was simply not her type and she felt well out of it.

***

At the hospital, Brendan was talking to Silvia. Alex had come early with her toiletries and Molly had sent a dressing-gown which she never wore and thought might be useful. 'Molly's not the dressing-gown type,' Brendan said, 'except in the depths of winter and then she's got an old army great coat that she's, um, decorated.'

'It's very kind of her,' Silvia said.

'Not really,' Brendan said, 'she's probably glad to get it out of the cupboard. I thought you might like to go and visit Lexy if you feel up to it. Good to have a bit of a walk.'

'Nice young man in the room with him,' Birdie chipped in.

Silvia looked at Brendan for confirmation. 'Bill Ferguson,' said Brendan, 'Lexy says you know him.'

'Not really. I've met him, that's all.'

'All the same,' said Birdie, 'might want to brush your hair.'

Poor Silvia went several shades of pink. 'I can't. I can't use my right arm.'

'Oh Brendan'll do it for you. Brendan's a great brusher, he's done mine often enough, haven't you dearie?'

Much as Birdie often drove him mad, Brendan could've kissed her that morning. Silvia's hair did need a brush. He attended to it and made her look quite presentable in Molly's gown and walked her off to see Lexy. Only halfway there did he realise that a catheter and a bag of urine were not the most romantic accessories a man could have. Never mind, he'd just have to do his best to keep them out of her line of vision.

Terence did not spend long with Emily. He made them both a cup of tea since Emily's arthritis was this morning so bad he could see that she herself wasn't really up to the task. Neither commented on the fact but Terence wondered just how long she would be able to go on living alone. In her own way, he thought, she was as stubborn as Artie Turner; it was just that she, somewhere along life's journey, had learned about grace under fire; Artie knew only how to whinge and complain.

'The man is quite impossible, we all know that. I mean, a wheelchair. It is not a fate worse than death, Terence. He is not, as I understand it, in a great deal of pain. He just wants to make life as difficult as possible for those around him. He has to be stopped.'

'Any suggestions?'

'Several. Most of them illegal.'

'So what can I do to help?'

'Pat's been invited to stay with old friends down at Somers. Do her the world of good. I thought maybe you could find an excuse to put Artie into hospital.'

'Normally there are one or two beds available for respite care. When is this supposed to happen?'

'In a few days.'

'Just as well it's not tomorrow, he'd be sleeping on the floor, the place is chockfull. You know what's going to be the hard part, Emily, don't you?'

She nodded. 'Oh yes. Convincing Pat. I'm sure Artie could always be rendered unconscious if it came to the crunch.'

Terence smiled to himself, considering what means he might use to knock Artie out if the necessity arose, as he drove out to Joneses. He'd phoned Molly from Emily's place, he wanted to make sure, tea leaves or not, that he wouldn't be treading on anyone's toes. And he wanted to preserve what was left of Alex Popovich's dignity. He felt, as Molly had done, that it had probably taken a battering from Bruce Cameron.

Terence explained the situation at some length to

Alex: the new vineyard he'd bought rather rashly, since he knew next to nothing about grape-growing; how he'd underestimated the amount of work he'd need to do to look after the place and how he was now, especially after the storm and with vintage so close, in a bit of a bind. It had occurred to him that Alex, at least in the short term, might be able to give him a hand – and the manager's cottage was still in decent repair, he could stay there.

'Oh, Alex, that sounds like a win for everyone!' Molly exclaimed.

Alex was quite bewildered at the speed with which his life was changing. 'If you really think I could be of use,' he said. 'As it happens, I do know a little about grapes. After the war, before I come to Australia, I work for a time in the Rhone Valley.'

Terence was starting to think that maybe Shirley's tea leaves had something going for them after all.

'When would you like me to start?' Alex asked.

'Well, Dr Bowen's holding the fort for me. We could go over to Eldershaw now if you like.'

Which is what they did. And Molly was left alone on the farm again.

The clinic wasn't busy that day; no doubt most people were too busy dealing with the aftermath of the storm to worry about their health.

Esme Watson did pop in to get something for her shattered nerves and to exaggerate the damage done to the point where it sounded as though the valley had been struck by a cyclone.

'The Billings lost their hayshed,' she reported. 'The whole thing crashed to the ground. It's a wonder no one was killed.'

'Esme,' said Shirley. 'That hayshed has been falling down for years. And it's in their top paddock. Why would anyone have been there in the middle of a thunderstorm?'

'I'm just saying,' said Esme, miffed, 'that a great deal of damage occurred.'

'Some, no doubt.'

'I suppose Dr Elliott lost all his grapes?'

'None.'

'Oh. Well that's a mercy.'

'It is indeed. Did you want to make another appointment?'

'I'll ring, Shirley, thank you. My nerves will let me know when I need one.'

Simon came out of his surgery after she'd gone, looking almost cheerful. 'You know, I don't mind the old bat so much any more. I suppose it's living alone that does it, I must watch myself.'

'Does what exactly?'

'Gives a person all these funny ideas. All these little prejudices. Makes them set in their ways. I think Esme might be very different if she had something useful to do.'

Shirley looked at Simon with new respect. It was not the sort of insight she expected from young Dr. Bowen. 'I think you could be right,' she said but Frank arrived bearing roses before she could take it any further. He had, it seemed, done all he could to find Michael Harris and to no avail; Burrigan had now taken over.

'Reckon he'll be halfway to Queensland,' Frank said. 'So I took a break and picked this lot. Storm ruined most of them but these were by the garage, got a bit of shelter.'

'Thank you, Frank, they're gorgeous,' said Shirley and dutifully went to get a vase.

'Oh, and I've got that recipe you wanted, Simon. For the master sauce?'

Simon seemed more excited than Shirley. Next thing

he and Frank were talking Chinese cooking and in no time at all they were planning a joint dinner party and Shirley had somehow agreed that it could be held at the Dean house, since Simon didn't move for another week and she had the most suitable kitchen. 'So long as I don't have to cook!'

'Absolutely not!' said Simon.

'You can sit under that pyramid thing and meditate,' said Frank.

Shirley wondered what Vicky would think. Especially when Simon announced his intention of inviting Emily Page.

At the hospital, things had gone well. Lexy was delighted to see his mother up and about and proud to let her know that he and Bill were now friends. 'You remember Bill, don't you, Mummy?'

'Of course I remember Bill, he gave us a new tyre for the car.' She smiled at him shyly.

'How are you?' Bill said.

'Oh. Not too bad. Fell off the ladder. Stupid.'

'Easy to do when you're dead tired.'

'Bill's pee's all going into a bag,' Lexy pointed out helpfully. 'So the doc can see how his kidneys are going.'

'Lexy!' said Silvia and to Bill, 'I'm sorry.' Bill just shrugged.

'Lexy,' said Brendan hurriedly, 'shall we go and get some orange juice?'

'Kids,' said Silvia after her son had departed. 'Sometimes you could just kill them.'

'He's a great little fella. The catheter – he was sort of fascinated, you know, so I explained it all.'

'Is it very uncomfortable?'

'Not too bad. Comes out tomorrow.'

'That's good.'

There was an awkward silence. Bill was thinking what a different sort of girl she was, different to Kerry-Anne anyway, who would have found the whole idea of a catheter disgusting. She'd hated hospitals.

'I had a proper chat to Lexy's grandpa yesterday,' Bill said finally. 'He's a nice bloke.'

'Lexy adores him. He's been good to me too. Kept things together since Janni died.'

'Your husband.'

'Yeah. Died three years ago. It's been tough. And now I'm not sure what's going to happen.'

'No more picking, you mean.' She nodded. 'Something'll turn up, Silvia. Maybe it's time you settled down. Got to stay in one place a while, I mean. Then Lexy could go to school. Bright little boy like him, he'd enjoy school.'

'I don't think he's ready for it.'

Bill thought, love it's you, you're not ready to let him go. But he just smiled. 'I guess a mum knows best.'

'The settling down in one place though … I wouldn't mind that so much,' Silvia said.

'Of course I don't mind!' Molly lied. She was on the phone to Brendan, who'd rung to say he was covering for Marta and wouldn't be home till late.

'You're quite sure?'

'The poor woman, she can't have had any sleep at all. Don't worry, I'll be fine.'

'At least Alex is there.'

'No, he's not.' And Molly filled him in on the change in Alex's circumstances.

Brendan was delighted. 'I suppose he'll want to tell Silvia himself.'

'I should think so. But anyway, I'll be alright, Shirley's calling in to bring some fabric, I'll see if I can make her stay a while. I'll see you, what – about ten, then?'

'Something like that. Oh, and Frank reckons Harris'll be interstate by now but you take care. You and Doris.'

'We will. Love you.' She hung up. Damn, she thought. She knew it couldn't be helped but she hated being alone at night. Maybe Brendan was right and they ought to get a dog. Or even a cat, that wasn't a bad idea, a cat might keep the rats down.

While Molly was considering the pros and cons of a cat versus a dog, Silvia Popovich was lying in bed worrying about more weighty matters, like where she was going to live and how she was going to feed her son. Life had always been tough for Silvia. Her father had died when she was very young and her mum ... well Silvia, trying to be charitable, supposed her mum had done her best but it had been a pretty second-rate best. Too much booze, too much time in front of the pokies. It was her grandmother who had rescued Silvia. And then, when she was eighteen and working as a waitress at the pub, Janni had come and swept her off her feet.

They'd had seven good years, Janni was a timber worker, he made good money, they'd even managed to put some by, dreaming of the day they'd have a place of their own. And then Janni was gone and the good years with him.

Silvia thought how grief and poverty had eaten away at her like a cancer, had deprived her of the energy to look for a better outcome. She thought she was weak and hated herself for it but felt helpless to change. And yet – and yet – Bill had lit a tiny candle of hope. Something'll turn up, he'd said. He was bright and positive like Alex tried so hard to be. She almost believed him. Then Alex was at her door.

'May I come in?' he asked. And he sat down and told her about his new job at Dr Elliott's vineyard and how they could all stay there for a while until they got on their feet because Dr Elliott needed his help with the vines. The candle burned a tiny bit brighter.

The radio was playing songs from the new musical 'Cats,' which was soon to open in London. Molly was humming along, she'd grown up with 'Old Possum's Book of Practical Cats' and she thought the show might well be a big success. And as she sang about the Jellicles she of course became more and more enamoured of the idea of getting a cat herself. She'd always loved cats – why hadn't she thought of it before? Her musings were interrupted when a loud banging started on the door – so loud she nearly jumped out of her skin. 'Hang on, Shirley, coming!' she called. But it wasn't Shirley leaning against the wire when she opened the door, it was Michael Harris. Not halfway to Queensland after all.

CHAPTER FIFTEEN

Harris looked ill. And dangerous. He tried to push his way in but adrenalin came to Molly's aid, she was too quick for him. She slammed the door in his face and drew the bolt and stood there for a moment, panting, terrified. The banging started again. She ignored it and ran to the phone. Bev eventually answered. 'Bev? Get me Frank Gilroy. Tell him it's urgent … No, I need him out here … Why? Because some junkie's trying to break into my house and I'm all alone, Bev, is that good enough? … Thank you.'

She hung up, shaking like a leaf now. Suddenly all was quiet. Somehow, that was more frightening than the banging had been. She thought to herself that Brendan was right, Dobermans were lovely. They should get one. She saw Brendan's golf bag in the corner and crept over and took out his number one iron. She stood there grasping it, waiting, feeling scared and foolish. Then the doorbell rang, piercing the silence. Molly shrieked – and then heard a familiar voice calling to her. She ran to the door, opened it quickly, dragged Shirley Dean inside and slammed it shut again. It took her a moment to explain what had happened.

'You're sure it was him?' Molly nodded. 'We'd better call Frank.'

'Bev's looking for him.'

'Then we'll just sit tight until he gets here.'

Michael Harris was now in desperate straits. He banged on the window but didn't have the strength to break it. He tried the door again and then saw the lights of the police car coming up the drive. Not what he had in mind.

Molly and Shirley saw them too, the flashing blue and red. 'Thank God,' said Molly.

'I'm going out to help him,' Shirley said. 'I don't suppose he's got any back-up and who knows what Harris is capable of.'

Molly felt emboldened by the thought of three against one. 'I'll come too.'

The noble gesture of the women proved unnecessary. Michael had tried to run and had collapsed after a few paces. Frank was already half-dragging him towards the car.

'We thought you might need some assistance,' Shirley said.

'No thanks, Shirl. She's right. You could ring the hospital though. This young idiot needs a doctor.'

'I'll do that,' said Molly.

'Just as well you got here when you did.' Shirley's voice was warmer than usual.

'All part of the service, Shirl.' Frank was clearly pleased to have won her approval, even if it was just for a moment.

Michael Harris appeared to have swallowed half the hospital pharmacy. The result was a spectacular overdose which almost killed him. There was nothing threatening about him now, lying on a hospital trolley, he was just another pathetic junkie. Terence, Simon and Brendan worked hard to save him, pumping out his stomach and putting up a drip to replace the lost fluids. Simon was puzzled at first; the kid was clearly an addict but where were the tell-tale puncture marks? It was Terence who pointed them out on the soles of Martin's feet. That was a first for Simon.

'They'll shoot up anywhere if they're desperate enough,' Terence said. 'I actually saw a girl once – couldn't have been more than sixteen – try to inject into her eyeball.' It was too much for Frank, who needed a small brandy to calm his already queasy stomach. He expressed surprise that alcohol was kept on the hospital premises but was assured by Brendan that it was strictly for medicinal purposes.

Fortunately two patients had been discharged that afternoon and there was a bed available when Michael was finally ready for the ward. He would be taken to Burrigan and charged with sundry offences the next day.

Brendan rang Molly as soon as he possibly could. 'Are you okay?'

'Now I am. But Brendan? Maybe we'll get a dog.'

'Good idea.'

'Will you be home soon?'

'About an hour.'

'I'll get on with some sewing.'

Molly tried to do just that, laying the pattern for Shirley's tai chi outfit on to the white fabric. She found herself jumping at every little noise until the rats in the roof started their nightly shenanigans. Then she forgot Michael Harris. And she forgot about Dobermans. 'A big tabby cat is what we need,' she said. 'A lean and hungry tabby cat.' She yelled at the ceiling. 'You hear that up there?'

***

For some in Wandin Valley, life became a little calmer in the ensuing days. Terence quickly discovered that he'd made a wise decision in employing Alex Popovich and even began to hope the older man might stay a while. Alex was full of encouragement and Terence needed that.

'You keep saying the place is run down, Dr Elliott. And yes, the cellar, the fences, these things need repairs. But the grapes are not run down, just look at them! And they were not even pruned so good. Is amazing.' Alex made Terence feel that he had not been an idiot after all, that buying the vineyard had been a wise investment.

'Alex, there's something else we need to talk about. Silvia's arm is healing well but she's quite anaemic, I want to keep her in hospital a while longer. Lexy though, is really ready to go home. Do you think you can manage him out here?'

Alex smiled. 'He will get bored ... but of course we will manage. If only Silvia would let him go to school.'

'I've got an idea about that,' said Terence and made a mental note to call and see Liz Anderson.

Molly decided that the best way to get over the recent unpleasantness was to busy herself with the farm. She wanted more livestock, especially since the arrival of piglets had now been indefinitely postponed, and it was sale day over at Harlow West.

'Goats,' she said to Brendan over breakfast. 'I love goats. Very intelligent. And *very* productive. Milk, cheese, meat.'

'Didn't Vicky say a cow would be more sensible?'

'Yeah, she did. I don't know why ... goats are so much more interesting.'

'I'll say it again. We need a dog.'

'Why? Michael Harris is in the lock-up.'

'There'll be another Michael Harris one day.'

'Do you want to scare me to death?'

'I want you to be safe.'

'Look. I'll go to the sale and see what's there, alright? See if there's anything appealing.'

'Exactly what I'm afraid of! You'll go and waste money on, I don't know, a camel. Such beautiful long eyelashes!'

Molly was hurt. 'I meant appealing price-wise, Brendan. Please don't treat me like some silly little girl from the city.'

'I'm sorry.' Molly did not melt. 'I'm really sorry. But you will try to get a dog as well?'

She was cool. 'Yes. Alright. A Doberman as well. But they may not have any. Or camels either. This is mainly dairy and sheep country, you know.'

Brendan tried hard to win her round. 'It's just that I've always had a thing about Dobermans. Ever since I was a kid. Actually … it might be best to get two. One dog becomes so dependent on you. Needy, you know? Two are company for each other.'

'Two then. A male and a female.'

Brendan risked his luck. 'Two males. Then we'll outnumber the females. You and Doris, that is.'

'Camels do have long eyelashes, don't they?' said Molly thoughtfully. 'Very pretty. And they're awfully good in a drought. Maybe I could breed them for the Middle-Eastern market.' Brendan had a horrible feeling she might be serious. 'By the way,' said Molly, totally changing the subject, 'how is your match-making going?'

'I have hopes,' Brendan said, 'but the wheels of romance turn slowly in Wandin Valley.'

'Tell me about it,' said Molly.

Needless to say, life had not got any calmer for Pat Turner. She was trying to escape for an hour to go to the hairdresser on this particular morning but Artie was doing his damnedest to prevent her.

'What if my wheelchair tipped over? I could be lying on the floor for hours, helpless.'

'Not hours, Dad, I won't be gone that long. And it's never tipped over before.'

'Happens all the time. You read about it.'

'I'm sure it doesn't, there'd be an outcry. Wheelchairs have to be safe. And please don't smoke while I'm gone, you could burn the house down.'

'Good thing if I did, you'd be rid of me. Go out all you liked then.'

'Dad!'

'Don't know why you're getting your hair done anyway, what's the point? You think it'll make some man take notice of you? Not a chance, lovey, you've missed the boat, you have!'

Pat left in tears. Emily Page saw her go and rang Terence Elliott.

Terence was having a busy morning. He'd seen a few patients and had called at the primary school. There he'd chatted to Liz and she in turn had enlisted the help of a very obliging Tiffany Brownlow. The three of them had come up with a plan, the details of which Terence had duly passed on to Brendan Jones. The game, as they say, was afoot. Now it was time to deal with Artie Turner, a slightly more complex problem but not insurmountable. Terence was normally an honest man but in his line of work a lie was occasionally called for, usually to allay fear or to lessen anguish or promote peace of mind. This particular lie, about the mistake in Artie's last lot of blood tests, the unfortunate mix-up in the results, was a pure fabrication and could have been classed as a sin – until you thought about Pat Turner's sanity. Then it became an act of charity.

***

Molly called at Vicky's surgery for some expert advice before heading off to the saleyards. As so often happens, the advice was not exactly what she wanted to hear.

'Goats?' said Vicky and shook her head. 'Not a good idea.'

'Why not?'

'Your fences, for a start. Any self-respecting goat would have her head through in a minute. Probably catching her horns on the way. And since very few goats are born with a reverse gear, where the head goes, the rest soon follows.'

'I can't afford new fences,' Molly said sadly.

'Then there's feeding – it's a myth that goats eat anything. Well they do if they're starving. But that's not the way to have healthy animals.'

'No need to go on. You've convinced me.'

Vicky smiled. 'Sorry, Moll. I like goats too. But you have to be practical.'

'Yeah. More's the pity.' Molly sighed and went on to tell Vicky about Brendan's desire for a couple of Dobermans. That was not well-received either.

'They're not country dogs, Molly. They were bred as guard dogs, they need an awful lot of training to be good pets. And they tend to have quite a lot of health problems.'

'Will you tell Brendan? He's got this little dream, see.'

'I'll tell him that what he needs is a female kelpie-cattle dog cross. Or maybe a border collie.'

'I might go to the sale anyway. Have a look around.'

'Good idea. See what's available, check out the prices. Give me a call if you need any more advice.'

'Thanks, Vicky. Oh, I forgot to ask – how was dinner the other night?'

'Just bearable. It's the dinner tonight I'm worried

about. If I grab some takeaway can I come out to your place?'

'Oh, it's the Great Asian Cookoff, isn't it?' Molly giggled. 'Love to be a fly on the wall.'

'God knows how it'll go. Two culinary egos at work. Frank is so earnest and Simon's such a show-off. You know he's taken up polo? Hey – maybe you should get Brendan to play.'

Molly laughed out loud at that. 'Only one problem – he's never been on a horse in his life.'

There were plenty of sad old nags at the saleyards, had Molly been tempted to get Brendan's riding career started. There were also a great many very appealing goats and a lot of sheep and cows. There was one cow, even sadder and older than some of the horses, that Molly seemed to keep passing. It was in a pen by itself and seemed thin and careworn. It was a Jersey, with sad brown eyes. Molly did not see any Dobermans. Or camels, for that matter. She bought a very good chicken sandwich from the CWA canteen, nodded to a couple of people she knew and thought to herself as she wandered around with her catalogue that she was starting to feel just a little bit like a local. It was interesting that the locals, in return, seemed more accepting of her outlandish gear than was once the case. 'Gawd, would you look at what Molly's got on today,' was about the extent of it.

At the hospital, Silvia was having lunch with Lexy on the verandah. Alex would be collecting him later in the afternoon; Silvia was relieved that he had made such as good recovery, that he had somewhere safe to go. She wished she was going too. She supposed it was necessary that she stay behind in hospital, Doctor Elliott seemed determined to keep her there, but she felt strangely unsettled. Lexy was very excited about seeing the vineyard but a bit concerned about his mum.

'Will you be alright in here all by yourself?'

'Of course I will.'

'I'll come and visit her.' Bill had arrived and indicated a chair. 'Mind if I join you?'

'Please.' Silvia smiled, embarrassed as always. 'Are you going home too, then?'

'He is, he's going tomorrow, Bill, aren't you? No more catheter, see.'

'Yes, I see,' said Silvia.

'Hey, good news about Doc Elliott's place. Lexy told me.'

'It's only temporary, but still.'

'Didn't I tell you something'd turn up?' Bill smiled. He wondered why she hadn't rushed to give him the good news herself.

Silvia had wanted to. But then she'd worried that he might think she was suggesting something, by saying she was staying on in the Valley. She wouldn't admit to herself in a million years that she didn't want to scare him off, that although she felt awkward and nervous talking to him, he was the first man since Janni that she could talk to at all and it was a nice feeling.

'It was good of Dr Elliott to give Dad the job,' she said.

Bill smiled and shook his head. 'That's not the way the doc put it. I heard him talking to Brendan – he said Alex was a godsend.'

'Oh.'

'A win all round.'

'I guess,' said Silvia.

'There's Tiffany!' yelled Lexy suddenly. 'What's she doing here?' Tiffany was indeed walking towards the hospital entrance with Liz Anderson. They disappeared inside and not long after Brendan brought them around to the verandah.

'Visitors for Lexy,' he announced grandly. Tiffany knew the Popoviches from the picking and Liz knew Bill so the introductions didn't take long. Tiffany, who was a very self-possessed little girl, explained that she'd been meaning to visit Lexy but wasn't sure how sick he was but then she heard he was going home so thought she'd better get in quick and Miss Anderson was kind enough to give up her lunch hour to bring her, wasn't that nice? Silvia thanked Miss Anderson who declared it a pleasure.

'You're not coming back picking then?' asked Tiffany of Lexy.

'Don't think so.'

'Then you should go to school, Lexy. Shouldn't he, Miss Anderson? Right here in Wandin Valley, you'd like it, honest, I know you would.'

Lexy looked doubtful and glanced at Silvia who, put on the spot, just smiled vaguely. It was Bill who spoke up. 'Well of course he'll have to go one day,' he said. 'Won't you, Lexy?' And Lexy actually nodded.

'Well if you do come to us, you'll be very welcome, Lexy,' Liz said quickly. 'We've got a great lot of kids in prep.'

'And hey, you could tell them about your cyst for show and tell!' Tiffany added.

'Oh, perfect!' said Brendan. 'So gross!'

Silvia looked unsure how to react but everyone else laughed and then Liz and Tiffany produced chocolate cake in honour of Lexy's recovery and after that Tiffany gave him a high five. 'I'll miss you, Lex. You too Mrs Popovich. But I might see you again next year. Especially if you go to school, Lexy!'

Silvia was quiet after they'd gone. 'Is something wrong, Mummy?'

Lexy wanted to know but she said she was just a bit tired.

'Everyone wants me to go to school,' Lexy said.

'We'll talk about that when I'm better,' Silvia said. 'When we know what's happening.'

'But aren't we going to the vineyard?' Lexy was bewildered.

'For now we are, yes. Lexy, don't worry, we'll be together whatever happens, okay?' She held out her arms and the child went to her and hugged her. Bill watched and thought Silvia needed love but so much more than that. She also needed to learn to love herself and to trust other people. Two hard lessons, no one knew that better than he did. He wished he could help her.

CHAPTER SIXTEEN

No one loved the old Jersey cow at the saleyards. No one went near her, stuck as she was near the other animals already consigned to the slaughterhouse. No one, that is, except Molly Jones who kept finding herself drawn to her pen where she stared at the cow and the cow stared back with warm, limpid eyes. She reminded Molly of kids in some Dickensian orphanage, or puppies in a pet shop window, pleading for a chance at a new life: take me, take me. A large figure loomed beside Molly.

'I hope you're not thinking of doing something silly, Molly,' said Bob Hatfield.

'Me? Like what?'

'Like buying that good-for-nothing cow.'

'Oh, Bob! Don't be ridiculous! Of course not.'

'Good. I hear things didn't go so well with the pig-breeding programme.'

'Disaster.'

'That boar of the Percivals. Useless lump of lard, from all accounts. Never mind, love, you'll have better luck next time, you and Doris. Give the old girl my commiserations.' He was hailed by a mate and moved on but when he looked back and saw that Molly was still with the cow he thought that she would assuredly buy it and it would all end in tears. Bob was amazingly prescient sometimes.

There was more than tears, there was another outbreak of hostilities when Pat announced to her father that Dr. Elliott needed to see them both at the clinic. Artie, as usual, was having none of it. He didn't care about his blood test results and he wasn't interested in Pat's need to get some prescriptions renewed. He wasn't going anywhere. Certainly not without a half-hour fight.

'You want to see the doctor, you go,' he said. 'Leave me all alone, why not? Get your hair done again while you're at it, looks bloody dreadful. If God'd meant you to be a blonde He'd have made you one. I'll go to that damn clinic when Doc Elliott's performing miracles, you can tell him that. When he's ready to get me walking again.'

'Why do you have to be so horrible, Dad? My hair's the same colour it always was, I just got it cut. Alright, stay here.' Pat did what she hardly ever did and headed for the car without him, she was almost at the end of her tether. And Artie realised just in time and agreed to go.

Emily, who tried not to eavesdrop but had no option since most of the conversation had taken place on the Turner porch, took it upon herself to ring Shirley and ask her to let Terence know which way the wind was blowing.

'Don't worry, Emily, there's enough of us here to handle Artie,' Shirley said, with a confidence she did not altogether feel since Simon had not arrived back from lunch. 'We'll see you this evening.'

'I'm looking forward to it,' Emily said. 'Two men showing off for us, I'm expecting gourmet fare!'

The dinner was in fact the reason for Simon's absence. He and Frank had been on a shopping trip to Burrigan for exotic ingredients not readily available in Wandin Valley and Shirley was doing her best to cover for him with more little white lies.

Terence showed a patient out and glanced at Simon's door. 'Is he back?'

'Not yet. A little emergency.'

'Ah, yes. At the – hospital?'

'Quite.'

It was then that Pat Turner arrived with Artie in his wheelchair. Terence took Pat straight in and Shirley parked Artie in what she hoped was a safe spot, near seventeen-year-old Jodi, who was hoping to see Simon.

'I'm sorry, Jodi, I don't know how long he's going to be, are you sure you wouldn't like to make another appointment?'

'No, that's alright.'

'But shouldn't you be in class?'

'Sport. I got excused.'

'Oh.'

'Good thing too,' said Artie. 'Gives you muscles in all the wrong places.'

'You think?' said Jodi and smiled at him, which an older, wiser woman would not have done. Artie wheeled his chair closer.

'Artie,' Shirley tried to warn him.

'Just having a friendly chat. Aren't we, gorgeous?'

Jodi looked as if she would like to back off but didn't want to be rude.

At the hospital, Brendan was collecting Lexy's few possessions together, including the frog that Alex had made him and some drawings that Bill had helped him to do.

'You'll have to come and see us, mate,' Brendan was

'When?'

'I'm not sure, today I hope. Molly was having a look at the sale.'

'Gee, a puppy.' He looked at Alex with longing eyes.

'Perhaps one day. When you are old enough to look after it. To make sure that it is properly wormed, yes?'

'If we're all set then,' said Brendan, 'better say goodbye. Then we'll go and see your mum.'

Lexy went over to Bill's bed. He was lying on top of it and sat up.

'Goodbye, Lexy. I reckon we might see each other again, don't you?'

'Can I really come and help you with the poddy calves?'

'If it's okay with your grandpa. I'll call round once I'm home again.'

'That would be nice,' said Alex and the two men shook hands and Bill and Lexy shared a farewell hug. Brendan hoped Bill meant it. He didn't seem the sort to make empty promises to a small boy.

They went to say goodbye to Silvia then and she told Lexy to be good and managed to be brave until they were gone. Then she had a little weep.

'Come on girl,' said Miss Bird. 'You'll be alright. There's that nice Bill Ferguson, he's still here. Bet he'll keep you company if you let him.' Silvia turned bright red at that and declared that she needed to rest.

The thing was that after Tiffany's visit, with her usual crash of confidence, she had decided that she was mistaken about Bill, that he did not see anything in her at all, that he no doubt considered her foolish and not a very good mother. They all thought that Lexy ought to be in school, they didn't understand why she needed this extra time with him, needed to keep the past intact that little bit longer. She sobbed into her pillow and Birdie, who was nowhere near as silly as some people thought, bided her time and let her be.

Unlike Birdie, Artie had never been droving and had never learned the patience that weeks and months in the saddle, staring at the rear ends of a thousand steers, teaches you. Artie didn't know what patience was. He jerked his head towards the door behind which, in his mind, Terence and Pat were involved in a grand conspiracy. 'What's going on?' he demanded of Shirley. 'Can't take them this long to work out how to poison me.'

Jodi giggled. Shirley glared. 'Don't be absurd, Artie. Pat had something she wished to discuss with Dr. Elliott. A medical problem of her own.'

'She's fit as a mallee bull.'

'If she is, it's no thanks to you. And how would you know? Do you ever give a thought to anyone besides yourself?'

Artie subsided, muttering about being unloved and unwanted. Jodie, who was a kind-hearted girl, took pity on him in a moment of madness. 'I'm sure it's not that bad,' she said.

Artie looked her up and down.

'You could make an old man happy,' he said. She looked a little startled. He pulled his wallet from his shirt pocket, took out some notes, put a couple back and held them out to her. 'How about it, girlie?' Fortunately for Jodi, Shirley saw the entire attempted transaction and was on her feet and out from behind her desk in a flash.

'Artie Turner! You revolting old man!'

While she wheeled him to the farthest corner of the waiting area, a white-faced Jodi was stumbling towards the door. 'I won't wait any longer, thanks. I'll come back another time. Maybe …' She was gone. Shirley turned on Artie in what could aptly be called high dudgeon. 'That poor child! How could you do that? To – to *proposition* her. Here, of all places. It's intolerable!'

Terence's door had opened. The doctor was standing there. Perfect timing. 'Did I hear correctly?'

'I'm afraid you did,' said Shirley. 'Young Jodi Thomas will probably need counselling.'

Terence didn't miss a beat. 'Artie, Pat's going to have a cup of tea with Shirley. And you and I are going to have a chat.' And before Artie knew it, Pat was thanking Terence profusely and he had taken her place in the surgery.

'Oh, Shirley! Did he honestly …?' Pat couldn't bring herself to say it.

Shirley smiled. 'You know something, Pat? We won't tell Artie but I think he might have done Simon a favour. I doubt if there'll be quite so many Year Elevens with mysterious ailments in future.'

Terence looked at Artie not entirely without sympathy. He could imagine what it must be like to spend one's days in a wheelchair, dependent on someone else for every need. He could also imagine what it must be like to be the 'someone'. To be Pat. So he had planned this meeting with utmost care. He had talked to Marta that morning. She had not been thrilled at the prospect but had agreed to find a bed for Artie – on one proviso.

'He has to come willingly, Terence,' she'd said. 'He'll be cantankerous enough, we all know that. Make him think he's Saint Arthur, doing a good and noble thing, perhaps that will help. Could you throw a severe medical condition into the mix?'

'I've come up with that one already,' Terence had said. 'That is – I can make it *sound* severe.'

'Then God help us, we will do our best. Anything so Pat gets a break.'

Pat had been the next problem. Pat was one of those people who did not see herself as deserving of anything. Much as she wanted to go and visit her friends Gwen and Robert, she did not see how she could leave Artie, she did not think it was *right* for her to leave him and go off and enjoy herself. He was her father and she loved him, even though he was a bit difficult at times. Shirley, however, had given Terence a bit of history; had told him how Pat had refused at least two offers of marriage and given up her hopes of a career in teaching. So Terence was in no mood to listen to excuses.

'Pat,' he had said patiently. 'You've just given your father sixteen years of your life. Sixteen uninterrupted years. We are talking about ten days now. A bit of R and R before you go totally bonkers. As your doctor I consider it a medical necessity. I really do.' Eventually reason had won.

And now there was just Artie. 'Well get on with it,' he said. 'I know why I'm here, you can break the bad news. You've hatched a plot the two of you, you're going to put me in a home.'

Terence almost smiled. Artie had just played right into his hands. 'As a matter of fact, Artie, we're trying to keep you *out* of a home.' That took the wind out of Artie's sails and Terence went on to explain that he was a little worried about Artie's last blood tests, all was not as it should be. Nothing too serious as yet but his haemoglobin was a bit low, probably not important, just a few days in hospital and he was sure they could sort it out.

'I get it,' said Artie. 'I go to hospital so Pat can go off to the beach with her friends.'

'You go to hospital so we can do some tests and stop you getting really sick. So sick that Pat can't look after you any more.'

'Very fortunate timing, doc.'

'Yes, isn't it?'

Artie glared at him.

'Tell me,' said Terence. 'Did you ever have a car just die on you?'

'What do you mean?' Artie was suspicious.'

'You know … just stop. And the mechanic took a look and told you the worst. Send it to the wreckers.'

'I did once,' said Artie. 'Old Ford. Done three hundred thousand mile. Great car, she was. Then everything went at once.'

'That's what'll happen to Pat, Artie, if she doesn't have a break. And who'll look after you then?'

It was a rather subdued Artie who wheeled himself out of the surgery. Terence followed. 'I hope you've got something decent planned for dinner tonight, girlie. Since it's the last edible food I'll be getting for quite a while.'

'Oh Artie, what are you talking about? The hospital food's excellent!'

'Doesn't matter anyway. I'm on my way out, according to the doc. Something wrong with my blood. I'll be dead in a month, more than likely. Now pay the bill Pat, and let's get out of here.'

'So he's not really sick?' Brendan asked Marta.

Marta shook her head.

'He's coming in for respite. Though Terence has had to imply some minor concern. And of course we'll give him a thorough check-up while we've got him. Do you know Mr Turner?'

'Only by reputation. Judy Loveday says he's impossible.'

'Judy is correct. Go home, Brendan, have a nice, peaceful evening, I'm going to need your help tomorrow.'

'No worries. Actually, I can't wait to get home, I'm

hoping Molly might have found some Dobermans at the sale.'

'You're going ahead with that, then?'

'Oh yes, definitely. I managed to talk Moll around. Such good watch dogs for the farm.'

Marta did not share his enthusiasm. 'So long as they stay on the farm. And don't attack someone's sheep.'

'Oh, but they'll be trained. They wouldn't!'

'They'd better not, Brendan. Or you won't be very popular. I'll see you tomorrow. Say hello to Molly. Tell her I'm coming out to see what she's done to the place when things quieten down.'

'Oh, she'd love that. You won't believe the changes. She's turned into such a farm girl, so practical and down-to-earth … tomorrow, then.'

Brendan's practical, down-to-earth wife was sitting by an old Jersey cow – she of the limpid brown eyes – in the Jones's orchard. Molly had actually paid good money for the cow; had paid someone with no compunction about ripping off the soft of heart (or head, depending on your point of view) to transport her here. And now Molly was trying, without success, to encourage the cow to eat. And that is where Brendan found them when he got home from work, looking forward to having a beer on the verandah and playing with his new dogs.

What ensued was not pleasant. Brendan was understanding about the Dobermans; Molly couldn't purchase what wasn't there. The Jersey cow was another matter. Yes, he'd agreed that she would run the farm. But a farm, not a palliative care hospice. Because no amount of TLC was going to cure that animal and make it productive.

'You're a vet now, Brendan?'

'It's so ill it's beyond being species specific, Molly.'

Molly hated that she had no answer for that. 'I hope you don't give up so easily on your human patients, Brendan. I hope you don't just send them all off to the slaughterhouse. Or maybe you do and we just don't hear about it!'

'That's a terrible thing to say!'

'Is it? Well I always thought you had more compassion than I'm seeing tonight!'

She stormed off to mix expensive feed for the cow. Brendan was left to feed himself after a ten-hour shift. It was their worst row – their first row – since they'd come to Wandin Valley and it wasn't over yet.

CHAPTER SEVENTEEN

Bill Ferguson sat eating his hospital dinner and thinking how quiet it was without Lexy chattering on in the bed next to him. Which inevitably made him think of Lexy's mum. Bill didn't know what it was that drew him to Silvia. Maybe it was just the fact that she'd been badly hurt as he had; that she, like him, did not have high expectations but tended to accept whatever life dished out. He smiled grimly. She may not have high expectations, he told himself, but that did not mean she'd be happy to settle for the likes of a lonely, rather dull dairy farmer. After all, what could he offer her but a roof over her head, a bit of security for herself and the boy? He did not imagine that would be sufficient. She was looking for something to light up her life as Janni had clearly done and Bill knew his star didn't shine brightly enough for that. And then Birdie appeared in the doorway. Bill's heart sank. He was not in the mood for rollicking tales of the droving days.

'I'm glad you've eaten your dinner,' said Birdie. 'It's more than that girl's done.'

'You mean Silvia?'

'Lying there, crying her eyes out. Poor thing, she's not had an easy time of it. Well I think I'll go and watch some telly in the patient's lounge. Just thought I'd let you know.'

'Thanks, Miss Bird.'

She left him to it. Bill shook his head. Subtle like a Bondi tram, was Birdie. But if Silvia was that upset, mightn't she prefer to be alone? He just wasn't sure.

At the Turner house Pat did chicken parmigianas, just like the pub. She didn't like them much herself but they reminded Artie of happier times and were one of his favourites. Nevertheless, he spoke little and just grunted when she asked what was wrong. Finally, after apple snow – another favourite because her mum used to make it – he looked at her and said, 'It's the thin end of the wedge, Pattie, isn't it?'

'Whatever do you mean?'

'Get me into hospital, from there it's just a quick ride with the ambos to the nursing home. And once I'm there you'll soon forget all about me. Just like Ralph Parker, his kids never go near him except at Christmas, he told me the other day on the bus trip.'

'That's not going to happen to you, Dad.'

'No? Well maybe you'd come and visit. But I'll bet you'll shove me into a home, the first chance you get!'

'Dad, I won't if you behave yourself. If you just meet me halfway, okay? So life's not too unbearable for either of us, is that a deal?'

'You promise?'

'Yes, I promise. But you've got to keep your half of the bargain.'

'Well I will, girlie.' He hesitated, as though suddenly overwhelmed by the enormity of the task. 'That is, I'll do my best.' For just a moment, he looked vulnerable.

For just a moment, Pat almost gave in and decided that it wasn't worth the worry, she'd cancel her plans. Then Artie gave her a little smirk. 'Hey. Who decides where halfway is?'

'Oh, Dad. Finish your pudding.'

Brendan was finishing some scrambled eggs when Molly finally came inside. She looked pointedly at the empty pan.

'Sorry. I thought you'd be spending the night by the patient's bedside. Would you like me to make you a sandwich?'

'No thanks.' Molly banged around making more noise than was necessary and made herself one.

'Did your friend eat anything?'

'What do you care?'

'I don't like to see animals suffering, Molly. I think she ought to be put down.'

'I didn't ask for your opinion. I'll get Vicky to see her tomorrow if she's not looking better. Have a nice evening.' She picked up her sandwich and a coat and torch and went outside again.

Brendan sighed and put his head in his hands. 'Oh, Molly. *Honestly!*'

The menu at the Deans' was somewhat more exotic and the atmosphere rather more convivial than at either the Turners or the Jones's. As so often happens, events which we anticipate with a degree of dread are often those which turn out to be the most enjoyable and that certainly held true for Shirley and even, to a lesser extent, for Vicky. At least, Vicky thought, Simon was too busy in the kitchen most of the time to be obnoxious and there was no doubt about it, the guy could cook. Well of course, couldn't he do everything?

'I was in Hong Kong a few years back,' said Emily.

'I remember having rice paper rolls for the first time and I'm quite sure they were no better than these, Simon.'

'I think your memory's playing tricks, Emily.'

'And as for Frank's satays!' gushed Vicky. 'Quite divine. Aren't they divine, Mum?'

'Very nice,' said Shirley.

'Plenty more!' said Frank and whirled off to the kitchen.

'The whole meal's delicious,' Terence said. 'Now you were telling us about the Alfred, Shirl?'

'Oh, I think we've heard enough,' said Emily.

'No, I'm intrigued.'

'Well I was only a few months into my training,' Shirley said. 'And Emily here was in charge of Casualty.

'I bet you all adored her,' Simon said.

'I should have said Emily *reigned* over casualty. She was variously known as the Empress or as Bloody Mary.'

'It's not an easy job,' said Emily in defence. 'All these scatterbrained girls just out of school, far more interested in the doctors than their patients. I felt more like a governess than a sister-in-charge!'

The stories of hospitals, of nurses and doctors past and present, continued unabated for some time. The illustrious line of Bowens featured quite frequently; Emily seemed to have worked with several of them. Simon was charming and attentive towards her; Vicky noticed how he discreetly slipped her a fork when her arthritic hands could not manage the chopsticks. Emily, in return, treated him – no, not like a son, Vicky thought. Like – a protégée. That was it. Vicky, who thought the world of Emily, did not know why it annoyed her.

As for Frank, he glowed every time someone praised his cooking, especially if the someone happened to be Shirley. And he liked the fact that Simon deferred to him in the kitchen. It was only a little thing but Simon got lots of brownie points for that – even, it must be said, from Vicky. Overall, the evening was progressing very smoothly. So far.

Bill finally decided nothing ventured, nothing gained. He got up, pulled on his dressing-gown, ran his fingers through his hair – and sat down on the edge of the bed again. He told himself that Silvia probably had visitors. And then realised he could walk straight past the door if she did. He could quickly ask if she needed anything and continue on his way if she seemed unwelcoming. He wondered why it had been so much easier to talk to her when Lexy was around. He went to the kitchen, passing the lounge where Miss Bird was watching the television and offered her tea but she had some already so he made two cups of hot chocolate and took them to Silvia's room.

She was embarrassed to see him at the door. She looked terrible, her eyes all red-rimmed, she did not want to see anyone.

'I was making hot chocolate. I thought you might like one.'

'Oh.'

He hesitated, he nearly went away. And then he thought, for God's sake, just go and talk to her, she needs a friend, you both do. 'Pity to waste it,' he said. 'You do like hot chocolate?'

Silvia nodded and Bill went in and pulled up the visitor's chair and sat down beside her. 'Been having a bit of a cry, then.' Silvia nodded again. 'I did a lot of that,' Bill said, 'when Kerry-Anne walked out on me. Does you the world of good.'

Silvia sat up and took her chocolate and they both sipped in silence for a while.

'Men aren't supposed to cry,' Bill went on. 'But I did. I cried because I loved her. I cried for the kids we never had. And when I was done, I realised I just had to get on with things.'

'Did she make you happy? When you were together?'

'No. I didn't see it at the time but that's the funny part. She didn't make me happy at all. She was very pretty. Beautiful, I suppose. She was Apple Blossom Queen the year we got married.' He paused. 'But she didn't make me happy. It wasn't like you and Janni, Silvia. At least you've only got good memories to pass on to Lexy. That's pretty special.'

'There'll never be anyone like Janni.'

'I guess not.' He got up. 'Well. I'll let you get some rest.'

Silvia could have kicked herself, why did she always say the wrong thing? She did not mean to drive him away but it was too late, he was at the door.

'Bill?' He stopped but she couldn't find the words. 'Thanks for the chocolate.' He gave her a little wave and was gone.

'I meant to tell you, Terence,' Emily was saying. 'Pat popped in for a moment this evening. Just before Simon picked me up. She's worried that Artie will change his mind tomorrow. Be difficult.'

'So long as Pat doesn't change her mind, we'll cope.'

'Artie's always been difficult,' said Frank. 'Since the accident, anyway.'

'He was difficult today,' said Shirley and told them about the incident at the surgery. There was some laughter.

'Getting senile, I reckon,' Frank said but Emily shook her head.

'It's not senility, Frank,' she said.

'It's attention-seeking,' said Terence. 'Of a kind. Artie's saying, hey, I'm still me, I still exist.'

Emily looked thoughtful. 'Though I doubt if he wants

to, deep down.'

'Exist?' said Simon. 'Well of course he does!'

'Would you?' said Emily quietly. 'Stuck in that chair, day in and day out, it's not like he has many resources to fall back on. He doesn't read much, or listen to music … he does like cards but he needs someone else to play. He likes the races but he needs someone to take him. So he sits there waiting for – what? Less and less independence. Until Pat can't manage and he has to go into a nursing home, the thought of which fills him with dread.'

'When you think about it,' said Vicky, not unsympathetically, 'if we were talking about a dog we'd all agree it should be put down.'

'Absolutely,' said Emily. 'The only humane solution. A dignified death.' She attempted to pull a plate of spring rolls towards her but couldn't quite manage it. Simon was quick to help. 'Which is what I plan for myself.'

The silence was deafening. Finally Frank found his voice. 'And how will you organise that, Emily?'

'Nothing messy, Frank. A simple overdose when the time's right. I've got it all worked out. I'm a coward when it comes to pain and I believe it's my right to end it. These are heavenly.' She dipped a spring roll into the sauce provided with obvious enjoyment. Simon stared at her, he couldn't think what to say, how to protest, but she deliberately avoided his gaze and turned to Vicky instead.

'Tell me, Vicky, what do you think about Simon's new hobby? You know, when I was a girl, most of the district used to play or at least go to watch. It was a bit like the Geebung Polo Club – "mighty little science but a mighty lot of dash" – and it often ended in a blood bath but oh dear, such fun!' And she laughed merrily. Strangely, only Terence joined in.

Soon after, Emily announced that she needed her bed, regretting that the wretched disease had ended her days as a party girl. Terence, who needed to be up early to fit in a visit to the vineyard, offered to take her home and after profuse thanks all round for a truly delightful evening, they left. In the car they talked of an aerogram Emily had received that day from Harriet and how she'd already managed to type back a reply. She told Terence how pleased Harriet was that he was keeping the name of the vineyard. They did not mention the little bombshell Emily had dropped at dinner.

It was avoided back at the Deans' as well, where Simon and Frank insisted on doing the washing up unaided while Vicky and Shirley were encouraged to enjoy a last custard tart.

'At least colonial rule achieved one good thing in China,' said Vicky, licking the last few crumbs of pastry off her fingers, 'though I don't suppose the Chinese saw it as a fair swap.'

'Hong Kong for a custard tart? Possibly not,' said her mother. There was some laughter at that but the evening was more subdued than it had been. Even the mere hint of an untimely end tends to put a dampener on things.

'Well I think we're all done,' said Frank at last. 'All shipshape again. I hope everyone enjoyed themselves.' The evening was pronounced a success. 'Nice to see Emily relax a bit,' Frank went on, ignoring any undercurrents. 'I thought she looked surprisingly well. She seems to have taken a shine to you, young Simon.'

'And it's returned.' Vicky couldn't help herself. 'But then who could resist all that flattery?'

Simon gave her a look. If they'd been alone he would never have let it pass. But he didn't want to make a scene in front of Vicky's mother. He managed to smile at Frank.

'She thinks I'm my grandfather reincarnated, that's

the problem. I'm pretty sure they once had a bit of a thing. During the war. God, is it that late, I really must go.'

He was careful to thank Shirley for the use of her kitchen and Frank for a great partnership. The two of them threatened Mexican next time. But he barely said goodnight to Vicky. He was hurt and it was obvious, no matter how hard he tried to hide it.

After he'd gone and Frank had followed, Shirley turned to Vicky and shook her head. 'I don't understand you.'

'That's okay. It's a mother-daughter thing.'

'No, tell me,' said Shirley. 'What is it that bothers you so about Simon's friendship with Emily Page? It's not like he's your boyfriend. And she's old enough to be his grandmother.'

'It doesn't bother me. I just think it's weird.'

'Why?'

'It just is.'

'Vicky. Emily was a great beauty in her day. I've seen photos. Men were drawn to her like bees to a honey pot from all accounts. But now she's living on drugs, she's in constant pain, she can't do many of the things that once gave her pleasure. But perhaps she can still enjoy the company of a charming and intelligent man, no matter what his age. And Simon *is* charming and intelligent, whatever you might think of him.'

Vicky shrugged. 'I still think it's – odd. You must admit Simon laps up the attention.'

'Simon hasn't been here long. Hasn't had much time to make friends. That's why he goes and visits his cousins. Plays mahjong with Emily. He's lonely, Vicky. And no, you're not expected to fill the gap, you've made it clear he's not your type. But try to be a little bit sensitive?'

Miffed at that, Vicky stomped off to bed. Shirley, who

thought her daughter was being unduly obtuse, poured herself a last glass of wine and got under her pyramid. Neither helped. And the evening had started out so well.

CHAPTER EIGHTEEN

Wandin Valley woke to another perfect autumn morning but to take the weather as an augury of things to come would have been most unwise. The stars had slipped their traces and quite a lot would go awry on this April day.

Simon, for instance, had barely slept. Simon had seen the after effects of attempted suicide in hospital often enough but he was fortunate in that he had never personally known anyone who had taken their own life or even contemplated it and the fact that Emily Page, of all people, might be doing that very thing gave him cause for deep concern. He arrived at the surgery well before they were due to open and went upstairs to have a coffee with Terence as soon as the latter returned from his visit to the vineyard.

'How are the grapes?'

Terence smiled. 'I sometimes feel as though people are enquiring about my children. They're well, thank you, Simon. Nearly ready.'

'Terence, about last night. What Emily said.'

'Ah, yes. I thought that might be why you were here so early.'

'Do you think she meant it?'

'I don't know. Maybe she did. Maybe she was just canvassing opinions on euthanasia. In which case we weren't much help. But I'm not going to ask her, Simon. I really don't want to know.'

'It just worries me deeply that she might be – you know – stockpiling drugs. Ones that we prescribe for her.'

'It's possible. We both know that you can kill yourself with paracetamol if you've got enough of the stuff. Hardly advisable but there it is.'

'Then *shouldn't* one of us talk to her?'

Terence was as serious as Simon had ever seen him. 'Please. Sit down and listen. And take some advice. You know the law. And you know Emily. You know her condition. It's getting worse. From her point of view, it's getting intolerable. Simon, she's a very intelligent woman whom we all love. Show her some respect. Allow her some privacy. Unless she asks you directly, leave this alone.'

Simon slowly nodded. Terence picked up the coffee pot and refilled their mugs. He hoped to God Simon had taken his words to heart. It wasn't as though he too wasn't worried about Emily. He forced himself to smile. 'And now I think we should say a little prayer for Marta. She's got Artie checking in today.'

Brendan did not make the same mistake twice and cooked enough eggs and bacon for both himself and an exhausted Molly.

'Did you get any sleep?'

'I'm fine,' was Molly's answer.

'And the cow, is she fine too?'

'She will be. You're going in early again, I suppose

you just want to get away from us.'

'We're busy, Molly. And we've got Artie Turner coming in. Not quite against his will but near as damn it. You think you've got a difficult patient, try Artie.'

'I suppose the family want to dump him, do they? Just like my cow got dumped. Past his use-by date.'

'You know nothing about it. He's a cranky old bastard. His daughter hasn't had a holiday in sixteen years. She needs a week off. I hope Vicky can help with the cow.' There was no kiss-and-make-up at the Jones's. Molly burst into tears the minute Brendan was out the door. He heard her and came back.

'Moll? Look. I just think that cow is a waste of time and money. Worse than that, I think you're prolonging her misery.'

'Do you? Well she ate some molasses and hot mash a while ago. So maybe not. And I just happen to think that everyone deserves a chance. Sick cows, cranky old men – all of us. Okay?'

'Sure. Bye, then.'

'Bye.' Of course they would have had a better day if they'd said sorry and thrown their arms around each other but Molly and Brendan both had a stubborn streak which sometimes overruled common sense. No doubt the stars weren't helping, up there running amok.

Artie had not yet arrived at the hospital, he was still driving Pat mad, playing the martyr at home. He kept discovering things she hadn't packed, like items of clothing he never wore, belongings he hadn't used in years, until his suitcase seemed unlikely to close.

'Just as well we're not flying, Dad, they'd never let you on board with all this stuff, you'd be over the allowance.'

'Well I don't know what I'm going to need, do I? It's not like there'll be anyone round to visit me. To get me any little thing I've forgotten.'

'The staff'll help you, Dad. They'd do any bit of shopping for you. Just got to ask nicely, people like to help.'

Artie grunted. A lot of it had been a ruse, to keep Pat running back and forth out of the room while he stashed more cigarettes into the case. He was done now. 'I guess I'll survive it all somehow. While you go living the high-life down at your fancy resort.'

'It's a beach shack, Dad. At Somers. You seem to think I'm off to the Bahamas.'

Marta would have settled for the Simpson Desert right then. Or anywhere. This day, so cool, so calm, so bright had started with Birdie falling in the shower and spraining her ankle. A nurse was with her and no one was sure how on earth it had happened but there it was. Birdie was being quite stoic, Birdie had fallen from galloping horses in her time, but she was confined to a wheelchair. Brendan privately thought that maybe a joust between her and Artie might enliven things in a day or two, with a little light betting on the side. He made a mental note to mention it to Marta when things had quietened down, if they ever did. This little reverie was interrupted by the arrival of Vicky, who needed to see Bill Ferguson and Brendan took her around. 'He's going home today,' he told her.

'I know, but this can't wait. And then Molly wants me to drop by, what's that about?'

'Don't ask me, Vicky. Please don't.'

'Okay.'

'She said it was a veterinary thing.'

'Oh it is. It is.'

'Right.'

They went into Bill's room.

'Got an early visitor for you, Bill.'

'Vicky. G'day. Nice to see you. Even if this is about a cow.'

'If it's about a cow,' said Brendan, 'I'll leave you to it.'

Vicky explained that Hal Secombe had rung her, he'd noticed when he was doing Bill's milking that one of the animals had a nasty gash on her leg. He'd left her penned and Vicky wanted to make sure that Bill was okay with her going out to check on it.

'That'd be great if you could, Vicky. I'm just glad Hal picked it up. Everyone's been so good helping out.'

'Just like you have when they've needed a hand, Bill.'

'I suppose. It's nice to have a good neighbours.'

'The country wouldn't work if we didn't.'

'Vic, can I ask you something sort of personal.'

Vicky grinned. 'How long have we known each other?'

'It's just … well it's been a while since Kerry-Anne walked out. That battered my confidence a bit, as you know. And I've been wondering … do you reckon I should just give up? I mean … am I still marriage material?'

It flashed through Vicky's mind that it just wasn't fair that some men, like Simon Bowen, waltzed through life with everything falling into their laps while a really nice bloke like Bill Ferguson should be left with so little self-confidence he had to ask her a question like that.

'Bill,' she said gently. 'You're quite a catch however a girl might look at it. You're a lovely guy, you've got a property of your own … my advice is to try asking! You'll be knocked down in the rush.'

Bill was blushing like mad. 'I was thinking about it, to be honest. But then …' He shrugged. 'I thought she was interested and now I'm not so sure.'

Vicky had a good idea who the girl in question might be. 'Perhaps she's feeling like you. Out of the game for quite a while, unsure of herself, you know? I wouldn't give up, Bill, not for a minute. Faint heart and all that. I'd better go and fix that cow of yours.'

'Thanks, Vicky. You're a real pal.'

Vicky laughed. 'Wait till I send you the bill.' She headed for the door and met Silvia coming in.

'Silvia! Hello. We've just been talking cows. How's Lexy?'

'Good. He's out at Dr Elliott's vineyard with his grandfather.'

'That's great. Let's hope you can join him soon.'

Silvia did not know how she'd be received and said the first thing that came into her head. 'She seems nice. The vet.'

'Vicky? She's the best. Been a mate for a long time. One of my cows has gashed its leg apparently.'

Silvia nodded. Standing there in the doorway she looked lost and helpless. Bill felt a sudden urge to protect her but he had no idea why she was there. 'Can I do something for you?'

Silvia plucked up all her courage. 'It's about last night. About what I said. I think I gave you the wrong impression. About Janni, I mean.'

'Silvia. It's alright. Of course there'll never be anyone like Janni. Not for you. There couldn't be. Sounds like it was a once in a lifetime thing. I understand that.'

Silvia whispered, 'Sometimes I can't remember Janni's face. I have to look at a photograph.'

'I bet you can feel him all around you, though.'

She nodded. She thought how sensitive he was.

'The question is,' Bill said, 'do you want to go on alone? Or do you take a risk. Let yourself get close to someone else. See if you couldn't make a good life with another person.' Silvia seemed to be thinking about that. 'I'm going home in a couple of hours. Done my time here.'

'It'll be lonely. Just poor Miss Bird for company.'

'Well I thought I might come back tomorrow and visit. If it's alright with you.'

'I'd like that.'

'Good. Might see if I can bring Lexy with me.'

'Thanks, Bill.'

Brendan, who saw the two of them together as he passed the open door, thought that maybe his attempt at match-making had life in it yet.

Vicky stitched up Bill's injured Holstein and then reluctantly drove to the Jones's farm. Molly had admitted on the phone to a lack of success with the Dobermans so at least she wouldn't have to fuss over two unsuitable dogs. But something told Vicky that Molly had nevertheless made a big mistake. She sounded far too eager and enthusiastic. And she smiled too broadly when she met Vicky's car.

'Oh, Vicky, thanks for coming. Just wait till you see her!'

Vicky would actually have preferred not to see 'her' at all. 'What is she, exactly?'

'Don't worry, I remembered what you said, I didn't get a goat. She's a cow. The most gorgeous little Jersey. She's in the orchard where I can keep an eye on her.' She was leading the way as she spoke. 'I admit she's a little bit out of condition but – there. Isn't she just adorable? With a bit of fattening up …'

Molly looked at Vicky, desperately hoping for confirmation. It was not forthcoming.

'Oh, Molly. What have you done?' Vicky gave the cow a quick going over and shook her head.

'She would have been sent to the abattoir, Vicky! Turned into pet food.'

'For good reason. She's got chronic mastitis, she'll never give you milk, she's too old …' Vicky stroked the cow's neck. 'You poor old girl, you've had it, isn't that right?'

'That's a terrible thing to say, it isn't right at all, I'm not giving up on her!'

Vicky sighed. 'I thought you were going to be practical, Molly,' she said gently.

'I'm trying. I haven't even given her a name … I just thought …'

'She could end her days peacefully in your orchard.'

'Something like that.'

'Okay. I'm going to be brutal. Give her some molasses –'

'I've done that.'

'Maybe try her on some green hay. But you're just delaying the inevitable. Sooner or later, she'll have to be put down. I'm sorry.'

Molly thanked her and thought, I'll show you, Vicky Dean. You and Brendan and Bob Hatfield and everyone. I'm going to nurse No-Name back to health. I'm going to make her as good as new!

For Molly the glass was always half full. She expected a miracle around every corner.

At the clinic Shirley was putting Frank Gilroy's latest offering of roses in a vase. They were magnificent yellow David Austins.

'A veritable sunburst,' Simon said.

'Poetry, now?'

'Hardly. They're just beautiful. And you have to admit, Shirley –'

'Please don't say it, darling. Don't say I could do a lot worse than Frank Gilroy.'

'The man can cook. His Peking duck – that was poetry if you like. As for his spring rolls – did you notice how many Emily ate?'

'She did enjoy them, didn't she? You know, I hadn't

seen her for a while, we've just spoken on the phone.'

'And you were surprised?'

'Yes. I shouldn't have been. I knew she was finding it hard to get around. All the same – I didn't realise how very bad her arthritis had got. These auto-immune diseases – they're very hard to live with. The pain, the isolation …'

'Exactly. Not everyone understands that,' said Simon.

The phone interrupted them. Shirley was glad, she didn't want Simon to ask her what she thought of Emily's announcement. The truth was she didn't think he'd like her answer. And she didn't want to talk about Vicky because she was still annoyed with her but too loyal to let it show. So she was glad to take the call.

'Wandin Valley Clinic, Sister Dean … Oh yes, Sheree … Oh, really? That's very good news … No, not a problem at all, I'll tell him. 'Bye.' She hung up.

Simon was on tenterhooks. 'Tell me it's true. She's cancelled.'

'She has. She's feeling ever so much better, she said. Just as I predicted – I bet she's been talking to Jodi Thomas,' said Shirley.'

Simon breathed a sigh of relief. 'Bless you, Arthur Turner.'

'And I bet it's the first time in a long time that anyone's said that,' said Shirley. Which at least gave them both a laugh.

'Terence was offering up prayers for Marta this morning. I wonder how it's going?'

'I'll go and help out myself,' said Shirley, 'if it means Pat Turner gets a holiday.'

'That seems to be the general feeling.'

'Such a nice woman. Pleasant, intelligent, a great gardener like Frank … and her whole life wasted on her father. I still think she and Frank would be such a good match.'

'*What*?'

'No, really. I mentioned it to Vicky the other day and she had the same reaction. But when you think about it, it's perfect! And Frank could keep Artie in line.'

Simon shook his head in amazement. 'One small problem, Shirl. Frank's besotted with you.'

'Oh, not really, he just thinks he is. And anyway, Pat's so much more suitable! I must see what I can do.'

What Simon could see was the hapless pair tripping down the aisle within a month. Someone should warn them.

CHAPTER NINETEEN

The man now marked as a possible future father-in-law for Sergeant Frank Gilroy was playing the victim as Pat pulled up outside the hospital. It was a nice hospital, painted white, with green lawns and shady trees surrounding it. There were flowers beds and a couple of swings for children.

'Prison,' said Artie. 'That's what it looks like and that's how I feel. Like a condemned man.'

'Please, Dad,' begged Pat. 'Don't make this any harder.' Somehow she got him out of the car and into his chair and was unloading his case when Brendan came running.

'Sorry, I was watching out for you and then a patient needed a pan, always happens.'

Artie glared. Pat smiled. 'That's okay, I'm used to managing on my own. I don't think we've met, I'm Pat Turner.'

'Brendan Jones. And this must be your dad. How do you do, Mr Turner, can I call you Artie?'

'You a doctor?'

'No, a nurse. Let's go, shall we?' Brendan carried the heavy case, leaving Pat with the easier task of pushing the wheelchair.

'Hang on, a bloke can't be a nurse, you look like a bloke.'

'Blokes can be nurses these days, Artie, you're out of touch. This is a very modern establishment, you're going to like it here.'

Artie shook his head. 'And pigs are going to fly. But lead on, young Brenda, take me to the lock-up.'

That was as close to bonhomie as it got. While Pat signed the admission forms in Marta's office, Artie sulked in his chair.

'She's going off on holiday, you know,' he said to Brendan. 'Gallivanting around the countryside while I'm left to rot in here.'

'As I understand it, Artie, you both need a break. This is a perfect opportunity. Pat gets to recharge her batteries and we get to recharge yours. Complete grease and oil change, that's what the doc's ordered.'

'I don't think I like the sound of it,' Artie said. 'Not one bit.'

'Wait and see. People go to health spas, pay a fortune for what you're getting. Isn't that right, Matron?'

'Quite correct, Mr. Jones. Now why don't you get Mr Turner settled, then Pat can go round and say goodbye.'

'Excellent idea, come on Artie, off we go. First stop, the west wing.'

'I hope you've put me in with a nice blonde.'

'Dad!' But they were gone. 'I'm sorry, Matron. He's incorrigible. I hope you can manage.'

'He'll be putty in Brendan's hands, don't you worry about a thing.'

'I feel guilt-ridden.'

'You mustn't.'

'He was saying he felt like a prisoner.'

'Some prison,' said Marta with feeling. 'He should try the real thing.'

Molly knew she ought to be finishing off Shirley's tai chi outfit. She'd promised to make it as quickly as possible and she did need the money. But here she was out with the cow, trying to convince herself that it had actually eaten some of the expensive green hay, that it was really looking a little bit stronger. Vicky would have told her otherwise; so would anyone less attached to the animal. But Molly had done what she had sworn she wouldn't, she had fallen in love with the wretched beast and its limpid brown eyes. She now had so much invested in it, emotionally and even financially, that she was quite prepared to sit by its side and will it back to health.

'We're going to win this battle, No-Name,' she whispered to it. 'But you've got to do your bit. You can't just curl up your hooves, you mustn't give in. You've got to fight. Do you understand?'

Had No-Name had the gift of speech, she might have told Molly that she simply had no fight left in her. But she didn't. So they continued in their fog of incomprehension, the girl weeping now and then, the cow bellowing frequently. It did not augur well.

Artie was in a room by himself for now, Marta had thought it was safest all round. Brendan was unpacking his bag and Artie was trying to repack it at the same time. The last thing he wanted was for Brendan to find his cigarettes.

'I'd leave it if I were you. I mean, I'm not sure yet that I'm staying.'

'Of course you're staying, I told you. You're going to love it here. Though I'm afraid I'll have to take these.' He'd found a packet of Artie's Marlboros and slipped them into his pocket.

'Hey! You can't nick my fags!'

'You'll get them back when you leave, you know you can't smoke in hospital. Now let's get you into some pj's shall we?'

'No.'

'Oh come on, Artie. These nice navy blue ones?'

'No. I'm on strike till I get my fags back.'

Brendan had dealt with recalcitrant patients before. And he had a sneaking sympathy still for this bitter old man. 'Artie,' he said. 'let's do a deal. Pyjamas and into bed, no fuss, or I tell Matron you're constipated.'

'But I'm not.'

'You're acting like you are. And Matron's a great believer in the old-fashioned enema. So …?'

Artie sighed deeply. 'You win, Brenda.'

By the time Marta brought Pat around to say goodbye, he was sitting up in bed in the navy blue pyjamas.

'Comfortable then, Dad?'

'I'm as miserable as a bandicoot on a burnt ridge, if you must know. But don't you worry about me. You go off and enjoy yourself. I'm sure they'll get in touch if I die while you're gone.'

Pat looked alarmed but Marta just laughed. 'You are not in the least bit likely to die, Mr Turner,' she said. 'Though you may drive Mr Jones to an early grave if you don't co-operate a little.'

'You will though, won't you, Dad? You'll co-operate? Remember our deal?'

'What deal was that?'

'Oh, Dad!'

'It's alright. I'll be good. Did you bring my shortbread? And my raisins?'

'They're right here. Beside the bed.' Pat turned to Marta. 'His little snacks, I can't make him eat fresh fruit. And he does like to have his tartan blanket.'

'Stop fussing woman, I couldn't give a toss about the damn blanket.' Marta gave Pat a tiny smile. She could imagine what would happen if the blanket disappeared.

Pat kissed him. 'Love you, Dad.'

'Go on, get out of here, go off and forget me.'

'I'm not going till Saturday, I'll see you before I leave for Somers.'

'Whatever.' He turned his back on them all. Artie could only cope with so much sentiment.

It was out of his way and he was tired but Bill decided to call at the vineyard on the his way home from hospital. He wanted to see how Lexy was getting on, Alex too for that matter. He found them in the winery, a bit of a misnomer at the moment for there was no wine. Alex was checking the old oak casks to see which might still have some life in them. Lexy went running to meet him.

'Hello Bill, what are you doing here?'

'I came to see you.'

Alex thought how good it was to see Lexy with this nice young man. After all, the child could barely remember his father and sad as that was, he did need someone.

'You are feeling better?' he asked Bill.

'Good as new. And Silvia's okay, I saw her this morning. I promised her I'd take Lexy to visit tomorrow. If that's okay.'

'Of course. He'd like that.' Alex made coffee and they walked around with their mugs so Bill could see the place. Alex said he had to remind himself he was not the owner, just the hired help.

'Did you ever have your own land?'

Alex smiled. 'No. I had three brothers, all older.'

'And they got it?'

'One did. The others, the war … you know.'

Bill didn't but he could guess. The Balkans had been

torn apart, he knew that much.

'This is really nice,' he said after a while, 'but the doc's got a bit of work to do.'

'Yes, but the vines are good. That is what matters.'

'True. Like my dairy farm – the house is nothing much and the fences need work but I've got a damn fine herd of Holsteins.'

'It is important to get the priorities right – the cows before the pretty house, yes?' Bill nodded. He was thinking, if only Kerry-Anne could have seen things like that. It was funny how everyday he was finding more and more things that had been wrong with Kerry-Anne.

Vicky came out of the post office laden with parcels for the surgery. She'd only been expecting one and here she was trying to juggle the lot and blow her nose at the same time. She was getting a cold and felt wretched; she just wanted to finish what she had to do at work, pray the phone didn't ring with some emergency and go home and crawl into bed. And of course – as Silvia Popovich had so recently discovered – men have a terrible habit of appearing when you least want to see them, when the witty, or in Vicky's case cutting remark, is least likely to spring to mind, especially since you've finally dropped one of the aforementioned parcels into the gutter.

'Allow me,' said Simon Bowen, deftly retrieving the parcel from the only puddle in the entire street. He then produced an immaculate white handkerchief and proceeded to remove the worst of the mud. Vicky could have killed him.

'Thank you,' she said, as nicely as she could.

'You sound terrible, Victoria. Getting something?'

'A mere cold. I'm going home to munch on some garlic.'

'How quaintly old-fashioned. Allow me to suggest two paracetamol and plenty of fluids.'

'A medical opinion, Dr. Bowen?'

'Actually, yes. Though you might add honey and hot lemon, my grandmother swore by it.'

'She who was married to the famous Grandie?'

'The other.'

'Then I might try it.'

'Can I carry these to the surgery for you? On the way you can tell me why you dislike me so much again. Or is it still? I thought we had a brief rapprochement for a day or two but maybe I was mistaken.'

'I don't dislike you, Simon. That's absurd. I just find you –' She broke off. They continued walking.

'You were saying?'

'I don't know,' Vicky admitted at last. 'I don't know what I find you. A trifle irritating perhaps. We just rub each other up the wrong way.'

'Well, at least you've been honest. And I promise I'll stay away from now on. We can all do without trifling irritations. Here we are, can you manage?'

'Yes. Thank you. Simon, that's not what I meant.'

'On the contrary, Vicky, I think it's exactly what you meant. Look after that cold.'

And he was gone, leaving Vicky with her parcels on the surgery doorstep. Just when she'd been about to relent and ask him in for coffee to see if they couldn't have an adult conversation for once. She felt like stamping her foot but it would have been childish.

At home, the first thing Simon did was to pour himself a sherry – he was acquiring a taste for it from Emily Page – and thought as he did so that he was picking up bad habits from Terence. But really, this town and especially some of its inhabitants were enough to drive anyone to drink. He did not think Vicky had been honest at all. Why hadn't she just come out and said that she found his friendship with Emily peculiar, to say the least? Peculiar because she didn't understand it.

Because with her awful inverted snobbery she saw anyone with two bob to rub together, anyone who'd been to a private school or who liked opera or God forbid, played polo was, per se, some sort of wanker. And then it dawned on him that Emily did or had done all those things and Vicky admired her greatly. He nearly prescribed himself some antidepressants but wisely decided he ought to talk to Terence first. He limited himself to one drink and spent the evening badgering the painters, who promised to finish in two more days, and catching up with his medical journals. It was worthy but hardly exciting.

Molly was becoming more than a little obsessive about No-Name. She'd begun to think that if she left the cow alone for too long it would surely die, that it was somehow her presence that was giving the old girl the will to go on drawing breath. So she'd dashed inside to take some sausages out of the freezer – well, she thought she had – but she had forgotten about Doris altogether until the sow's insistent oinking gradually impinged on her brain.

'Good grief! Poor Doris!' She was still mixing pig food when Brendan got home. He was not in the best of moods. There had been, just before he left work, another altercation with Artie. Brendan had found him smoking and had taken the cigarette. Artie said it was cruel to deprive him of his only pleasure in life. Brendan had offered a hot shower to ease his aches and pains instead and Artie had finally agreed, only to turn the shower hose on Brendan at the first opportunity.

'I've had it, Moll. I mean, he really is a monster. Are you coming to have a beer with me, I need to relax.'

'I'll just finish feeding Doris, and check on No-Name and I'll be in.'

'Still alive, then? The cow?'

'Yes! Doing okay.' Molly was a bad liar and Brendan got the picture but refrained from comment.'

'Good. I'll go and change then. What's for tea?'

'Sausages. I took them out – oh, my God.'

'What?'

'I *meant* to take them out of the freezer. But I might have forgotten.'

'Eggs, then. Great.'

Brendan did not throw a tantrum like Artie. But a tiny one was raging inside his head. When was Molly going to see sense about that damn cow?

Pat popped over to Emily's that evening to thank her for her support. She found Emily going through old photos.

'That's something I keep telling myself I ought to do. Sort them all out. Not that it really matters. There's no one else who'd be interested.'

'You will be when you're old like me, Pat. They jog your memory. And anyway, haven't you got a niece?'

'Over in Perth. Haven't seen her in ever so long.'

'Maybe you'll get over there one of these days.'

'Let's just start with Somers.'

'So you're all set?'

'Oh yes, I'm nearly packed. Nothing's going to stop me now.' She actually laughed. 'Not unless Dad burns the hospital down.'

Emily was privately thinking that she wouldn't put it past Artie, he'd do it just to ruin his daughter's joy, when Frank arrived, looking for her.

'Knocked on Pat's door and then I heard the voices,' he said as Emily let him in.

'Just in time for a sherry,' Emily said. 'We're celebrating Pat's liberation.'

'In that case I will join you, just a little one, but let me get it, Emily,' Frank said. He had, it turned out, come to see Pat. Knowing that she was also a keen gardener, he wondered if anyone was looking after the place in her absence and offered to do any watering that might be necessary. Pat was quite overwhelmed by his thoughtfulness.

'Well I'll give it a good soak before I go, of course … but if we don't get any rain … if you really wouldn't mind …'

'Consider it done,' said the gallant sergeant. He did not tell her it had been Shirley's suggestion – something Emily already suspected.

'And how's Artie coping at the hospital, have you heard?'

'Alright, I think. He's grumpy, of course.'

'I'm sure he's fine. After all, I haven't been called in to arrest him yet!'

No, thought Emily. But it's only day one. Later, after Frank and Pat had both departed, she managed to get herself some soup and then went back to the photos. She'd intended to spend the evening writing letters – or rather typing them, which she found much easier these days – but she decided they could wait. There were so many photos … and she was so young. And yes, it had been heaven to be alive. She thought of Pat, whose youth had been wasted, opportunities snatched away from her. It wasn't fair but that was life. She thought she could see what Shirley Dean might have in mind but didn't think it would work. She was pretty sure that Shirley knew it wouldn't work either.

At the hospital, patients were settling down for the night. Artie grizzled and complained about the uncomfortable bed for a while but then, to everyone's surprise, passed out and slept like a baby.

Birdie, who never slept much, lay wondering whether or not to try and talk to Silvia. Eventually she thought she couldn't really do any harm.

'You're tossing and turning a lot, dearie, what's the matter?'

'I can't sleep.'

'You want me to call the nurse?'

'I'm fine. I'm sorry if I disturbed you.'

'No, no, that's alright.' Birdie paused. 'You worry too much.'

'I've got a few problems, Birdie.'

'I've got a feeling they're all going to be sorted out, you know that?'

'I don't see how.'

'You're like that chappie in Shakespeare, what's his name, couldn't make decisions?'

'I don't know much Shakespeare.'

'I used to read on the track. Always took a new book along, you got a lot covered over the years. Hamlet, that's the one. You've got to make up your mind. Like – are you going to say yes when Bill asks you to marry him?'

'He won't ask me, Birdie. That was just a silly dream. Why would he want to marry me? His first wife was Apple Blossom Queen.'

'I remember Kerry-Anne. Selfish little bimbo.'

'He said she was beautiful.'

'Maybe she was. And about as useful as a bucket under a bull.'

'I think I'll go to sleep now, Birdie.'

'Night, then dear.' Birdie sighed. She hoped Bill Ferguson had a bit of get up and go. From the looks of things, he was going to need it.

CHAPTER TWENTY

The next morning, when Vicky dragged herself out of bed, she found her mother practising tai chi in the living room.

'Have you ever counted them all up?'

'What?'

'Your fads? All the things you've tried and discarded over the years?'

'I have an enquiring mind, Vicky. You should be grateful. It may prevent me from going ga-ga in my old age.'

'Some might say it's too late.'

'And some might say you should go back to bed and try getting out on the other side.'

Vicky got a box of tissues, pulled a waste-paper basket close and flopped on the couch. 'You'll miss me when I'm dead,' she said.

Shirley frowned. She went and put a hand on her daughter's forehead. 'That's quite a temperature. You are definitely going back to bed.'

'It's just a cold.'

'It's a bad cold. I'll get you some paracetamol.'

'I have to go to work, Mum.'

'Don't be ridiculous, darling. Go back to bed now. A hot lemon drink won't hurt either. Go on, I'll bring it in to you.'

Vicky actually giggled. 'Simon's grandma believed in hot lemon. He told me.'

'I thought you weren't speaking to him?'

'I'm not. I can't stand him.'

'Go to bed, darling.'

Vicky went. Shirley sighed. 'Delirious,' she said and went out to pick some lemons.

Terence was doing his hospital rounds. He was chatting to Silvia while he checked her arm. It was healing beautifully.

'I don't think the scar will be too bad. You can make up some exotic story about being set upon by bandits in – where? Mexico? Peru?'

'Bondi?' added Marta.

They were pleased that they managed to bring a smile to Silvia's face. 'Have you made any plans for the future yet?' Terence went on. 'You know you're welcome to stay at the vineyard for the time being if that's a help.'

'That's very kind.'

'I don't want to lose your grandfather.'

'You know she's got a suitor, doctor,' Birdie piped up from the other side of the curtain.

'And I'm sure we'll all hear about that when Mrs. Popovich wants to tell us, Birdie.'

'There'll be wedding bells before long, you mark my words.' But no one actually heard her words; they were drowned out by an almighty crash from a nearby room.

'Excuse me.' Marta was gone.

It was Artie, of course, with his breakfast all over the floor where he had swept it, tray and all. Brendan was for once not in the least amused.

'That's it, Artie.'

'Mr Turner, to you.'

'*Mr* Turner! You've gone way too far this time.'

'I take it,' said Marta icily, 'that this was no accident?'

'No it wasn't,' said Artie, defiant. 'Brenda brought me the wrong meal. Then tried to make me eat it!'

'I brought you breakfast. I'm sorry if you wanted Eggs Benedict but this isn't the Wandin Valley Hilton.' He shook his head at Marta. 'I'll get something to clean it up.'

'You're a wicked old man,' said Marta. 'Nurse Jones has been so patient with you. So kind. And you treat him – all of us – as if we're your servants. You're like a bad-tempered child. No, like the bully in the school playground.'

For some reason that got to Artie. 'You don't mean that.'

'I do mean it.'

Terence had been listening in the doorway. Now he entered the fray. 'Can I help here at all?'

'Yes, doctor. You can explain to Mr Turner that if he doesn't behave I'll arrange to have him transferred to Burrigan. Matron Arrowsmith runs a very tight ship indeed, she won't put up with his nonsense for a second.'

Marta went and Terence pulled up a chair, being careful to avoid the mess on the floor. 'What's going on? I thought you and Pat had a deal?'

Artie just shrugged.

'Artie,' said Terence gently. 'I know it's tough – '

'You haven't a clue.'

'I think I do. My work makes sure I'm reminded everyday.'

'You're just an onlooker, doc. It hasn't happened to

you. You're not stuck in a wheelchair. You're not old. You're not knocking on the door of God's waiting room.'

'Not yet. But it happens to all of us.'

Artie wasn't listening to Terence. 'I went to the bathroom this morning. Looked in the mirror. You know what I saw? A stranger. Who are you? That's what I thought. Because it creeps up on you, see. All the things you've been trying to keep at bay. It's like that little boy with his finger in the dyke, remember that story? Well I'm like him. I'm fighting till the end, you hear me?' And he rolled his wheelchair forward over the remains of his breakfast in a painful show of defiance. Terence said nothing. At that moment, he felt an aching pity for Artie Turner.

No-Name the cow was a lot closer to the end than Artie yet Molly was not about to accept her fate either, in fact Molly was still desperately trying to convince herself that No-Name's problem was not old age but some disease, an infection or a virus or a vitamin deficiency, something for which a simple cure could surely be found.

Molly was listening to her heart instead of her head again for No-Name was now lying on the ground in a most unnatural position, breathing with difficulty, and could not or would not get up. Molly went inside and rang Vicky but all she got at the surgery was the answering machine. In a way she was glad; it gave her a bit more time for the miracle to happen. She left a message asking Vicky to come as soon as possible and returned to sit by the little Jersey cow.

Artie's room had been scrubbed and polished. So had Artie. He was sitting in his chair, all alone, waiting for something to happen, someone to come. Maybe Pat, she'd said she'd call in. Though if she did they'd only argue. He found his secret stash of fags and lit up and sat there smoking for a while, taking perverse pleasure in dropping the ash on the freshly washed floor. Then he heard voices in the corridor outside and footsteps coming towards his door. In a panic, he looked around for somewhere to dispose of the cigarette. The linen basket caught his eye and he flicked it in there just as Brendan stuck his head in.

'Is the ceasefire holding? Or do I need a flak …' He trailed off. He was sniffing the air. 'For God's sake, Artie.'

'What?'

'You've been smoking again.'

'Me?'

'Oh, please. Don't come the innocent, I can smell it! And there's ash all over the floor, look!'

'Dust. Terribly dusty in here. Shocking for a hospital.'

'What did you do with it?'

'Nothing. Didn't have it. You stole them all, remember?'

Brendan wondered if it was worth another fight and decided he couldn't face it. 'Okay. I suppose if you want to destroy your lungs I can't really stop you. But at least you're going to get some vitamin D, like it or not. He wheeled Artie out without further ado.

When Bill went to collect Lexy from Terence's vineyard, the little boy came running to greet him as he had the previous day. His grandfather sent him to get a coat.

'He is very taken with you, Bill,' Alex said. 'He talks about you all the time. He is coming to expect perhaps too much.'

Bill understood what the old man was trying to say. 'I shouldn't worry,' he said. 'So long as you stay in the

Valley, I'll keep an eye out for him. And whatever happens, kids are pretty resilient, don't you think?'

'I hope you are right. Our future – it is still very uncertain.'

Bill smiled. 'That's true for all of us.'

When Lexy returned, he had a favour to ask. He wanted Bill to talk Silvia into letting him go to school. Bill looked at Alex.

'I am guilty of encouraging this,' Alex said. 'His mother will not be pleased.'

'Phew,' said Bill. 'No. I don't think she will.'

'But you'll help?' Lexy asked. 'She'll listen to you.'

How to get out of this one, Bill thought. 'Let's just take it easy, shall we? Softly, softly, okay?'

Lexy nodded solemnly.

Bill parked the ute at the hospital and bumped into Pat Turner as he and Lexy walked across the lawn.

'How's your dad, Pat?'

'He seems to have settled in. I'm actually going on holiday, would you believe. Just for ten days, but I am looking forward to it.'

'Well if anyone deserves it, you do. Oh – this is Lexy. His mum's a patient, we're –' He broke off suddenly. 'Good Lord, is that smoke?' Pat looked too. A thick cloud of smoke was coming from the west wing of the hospital. Closer to them, Miss Esme Watson was just leaving the building. 'Miss Watson! This is Lexy. There's a fire, look after him, can you?'

'Of course, Bill. Lexy is it? Goodness gracious!'

'Bill!' Lexy did not want to be left.

Pat was already running towards the building. 'I've got to help Mummy, mate. Be brave. Show her you're ready for school.'

Slightly bewildered, Lexy nodded and Bill sprinted off towards the main door.

Inside, there was ordered chaos. A fire alarm sounded constantly, drowning out the patients' bells. Marta was on the phone to Bev, trying to explain the urgency of the situation, while Brendan grabbed the extinguisher from her office.

'Yes, Bev, of course we need the brigade! … Right now, this is an emergency! … Thank you!' She hung up and turned to Brendan. 'Where is it?'

'Room Three, I think, judging by the smoke.'

'We have to get everyone out.'

Pat appeared. 'My dad, where is he?'

'On the verandah, Pat,' Brendan said and fled.

Artie was indeed on the verandah. He thought to himself it was getting crowded there and nurses kept bringing more patients out, darn it. He wasn't in the mood for yakking on, he wanted a bit of peace and quiet. And what the hell was that damn alarm?' Then Pat was tugging at his sleeve.

'Are you alright, Dad?'

'Of course I'm alright, if it's alright to starve because the food's inedible and not get a wink of sleep because the bed's –'

'Dad! For heaven's sake, there's a fire!' She turned his chair around. 'Look at the smoke! Can't you smell it? I suppose you smoke so much, you wouldn't know the difference! I hope they get everyone out alright …'

'Course they will.' But for just a moment, as someone inside called out for help, a worried expression crossed Artie's face.

Birdie was sitting on the edge of her bed. She couldn't walk with her injured ankle and seemed unfazed by the ever-thickening smoke. Silvia, who had been in the bathroom when the alarm went off, came rushing back. 'Come on Birdie, we have to get out.'

'Don't worry about me dear, you look after yourself.'

'Don't be silly, there's a fire, I'm not leaving you

here!' Silvia tried to pick Birdie up but it was beyond her. 'Where's your wheelchair, didn't you have a wheelchair?'

'I couldn't manage it, dear, not with the lupus, no strength in my arms any more.'

'Well lean on me, come on, we can do it, hop, it's not far, come *on,* Birdie!' The room was filling with smoke, they were both coughing, and Silvia was almost in tears. Then suddenly a strong pair of arms picked Birdie up. 'Are you okay, Silvia?' Bill asked.

'Fine.'

'Good girl. Let's go, then.' And he led them out.

Brendan, meanwhile, had found the seat of the fire in the laundry basket. It had spread to the curtains which, he noted, were highly flammable. He was in time to stop it spreading further and was putting out the last of the flames when one of the other nurses arrived. 'I think we can tell Marta to cancel the fire brigade,' he said. 'Not as bad as it looked, thank God.'

Some time later, Pat Turner stopped him in the corridor. 'Could I have a word with you, Nurse Jones?'

'Brendan, please. Of course you can. Come in here.' He took her into the office. 'It's about Artie, is it?'

Pat just nodded and sank on to a chair.

Bill and Silvia deposited Miss Bird on the verandah and then went to rescue Lexy from the care of Miss Watson. Actually, they seemed to be having quite a nice time together, sitting under the old pepper tree.

'Is everyone alright?' Esme asked. 'Such a lot of smoke.'

'But not too much damage,' Bill said. 'Nowhere near as bad as it seemed.'

'Well that's a blessing.'

'Thank you for taking care of Lexy,' Silvia said.

'It was my pleasure. Such a nice, polite little boy.'

'Miss Watson told me all about when she was a little girl,' said Lexy. 'They didn't even have television, I thought she was teasing.'

Esme took her leave, anxious to offer her services to stricken patients. Bill watched her go and smiled.

'Everyone gives her a hard time but she's not a bad old stick.' He turned to Lexy. 'Your mummy was very brave,' he said. 'She helped to rescue Miss Bird.'

'Really?' Lexy demanded a blow by blow description and then he wanted to know if Bill had talked to Mummy about you-know-what.

'Lexy,' Bill said. 'Give me a break. We've been dragging people from burning buildings. Not much time, you know?'

''Spose not.'

'As a matter-of-fact, there's a couple of things I need to talk to her about. Why don't you go and play on the swings for a bit?'

Lexy seemed to sense that it might be a good idea to go along with this suggestion. He went. Silvia smiled. 'What was that all about?'

Bill took a deep breath. 'I wanted to ask you if you'll marry me. Lexy wants to know if he can go to school. A yes and a yes would make us both really happy.' Silvia stared at him, speechless. 'But *your* happiness, that's the most important thing.'

Silvia was still speechless. But she managed to throw her arms around him and burst into tears. Lexy saw it and nearly fell off the swing into the rose garden. The biggest grin spread across his face. Oh wow, he thought. We're going to stay! Wait till Grandpa hears!

But there was not good news for everyone. Artie, still on the verandah though most other patients had been returned to their rooms, was pretending to be asleep. A brokenhearted Pat came and pulled a chair close to him and ordered him to wake up. She was angry but she did not shout, she did not want anyone else to hear. Artie made a good show of coming out of a deep snooze.

'Oh come on, Dad, I'm not in the mood. Not even you could sleep through a fire – especially when you probably started it!'

'Eh? That's a terrible thing to say, that's slanderous! Of course I didn't!'

'You've been lying to me. Said you hadn't had a fag since you got here.'

'Neither I have.'

'Not what I've been told, Dad. Apparently you've been lighting up at every opportunity. Brendan caught you smoking just before the fire started.'

'He said he smelled smoke, that's all. No proof it was me.'

'It started in your dirty linen basket, Dad. How do you account for that? Do you realise someone could have died? Lots of people could have died! Burnt to death and it would have been all your fault! Not that you give a damn, no one matters but you. You might be my father but you're still the most uncaring, the most self-centred old bastard on the face of this earth.'

'That's harsh, girlie. That's real harsh.'

'The truth often is. And now we're going to see the Matron. So you can tell her what you did.'

'No.' Artie planted his feet. 'She'll kick me out and you'll put me in a home.'

'Lift your feet up, Dad. 'Or so help me, I'll break them.'

Artie had never heard Pat sound like that. Implacable, that was it. He lifted his feet.

193

CHAPTER TWENTY-ONE

Esme had popped into the clinic to give Shirley an update on the great hospital fire. 'So very fortunate there weren't any fatalities. That some joy came out of the catastrophe.' Esme, it seemed, had already heard that Bill Ferguson – quite the hero – was going to marry Silvia Popovich, now wasn't that lovely?

Shirley couldn't let it go. 'But Esme, wasn't she one of the pickers?'

'Well maybe she was for a week or two, but she's a very nice person with a dear little boy and I'm sure she'll make Bill an excellent wife. Better than that flibbertigibbet, Kerry-Anne. Goodness, is that the time? I must rush.' And rush she did, at such a pace she almost knocked Simon over as he showed a patient out of his surgery.

He raised an eyebrow. Shirley shook her head and answered the phone. 'Hello Wandin Valley Clinic – Molly. What is it, what's wrong? … Oh, I see. Well she's home in bed sick, that's why you can't get her … Do you want me to ring her pager? … You're quite sure? … Well it's just a bad cold, if you change your mind …' Shirley hung up after a few more reassurances. 'Oh dear. I'm still not convinced that Molly's cut out to be a farmer.'

Simon sighed. 'It's not the cow? Brendan told me about the cow. Sounds like it needs to be put down.'

'Yes. And Molly will never do it. Not in month of Sundays. Oh, there was a call for you from the painters. They're finished.'

'Honestly?'

'That's what they said.'

'Oh frabjous day. I'll move at the weekend. Bye, bye, motel.'

Shirley laughed. 'I thought you'd be in the house tonight!'

'No, imagine the smell. Besides, I've got something on tonight. Saturday first thing. You won't know me, I'll be so much nicer when I'm out of that damn unit!'

Bob had called in to see Molly and found her trying to entice No-Name to her feet.

'It's no good, Moll. Once they go down like that they never get up again. You need the vet.'

'The vet's sick.'

'Vicky is?'

'Just a cold. But I can't drag her out here when she's not working. And the other vet can't come till tomorrow. There's got to be *something* I can do!'

'Have you got a gun?'

Molly looked at him in horror.

Bob was gentle. 'Maybe you should think about getting one, love. Just for emergencies. Sorry I can't help. Genny alright, is it?'

Molly could only nod. Bob went, but being Bob, he didn't leave it there.

***

Marta and Brendan were discussing the aftermath of the fire. 'Sergeant Gilroy's bound to ask awkward questions. I'm not sure how much to tell him,' Marta said.

'As little as possible?'

'That's probably best.' She smiled wearily. 'Congratulations, by the way. On your matchmaking.'

'I can't take much credit,' Brendan said. 'No more than Birdie, anyway. They did most of it themselves.'

Pat arrived in the doorway with a very subdued Artie.

'Miss Turner,' said Marta. 'Is there a problem?'

The fight was going out of Pat already; resignation took over as all hope of the longed-for holiday disappeared. 'Dad can't stay here. It's impossible. He has to be supervised. I'm going to pack his things. While I do, he's got something he needs to tell you.' Pat was gone before they could stop her.

Marta looked at Brendan. 'Does Dr Elliott know about this?' Brendan just shrugged. He turned to Artie.

'What was it you wanted to say, Artie?'

Artie was agitated. 'I don't want to say anything! I don't want to leave either. If I do, she'll put me in a home. That's what she's got in mind, I know it is!'

'Artie, we know the fire started in your room. Is that what Pat wanted you to tell us?'

'It was an accident. Do you think I'd do a thing like that on purpose? I just wanted a fag, that's all. I get desperate for them. It's about the only pleasure left to me, smoking. But I knew if I got caught you'd be mad as hell. So I flicked it in the bin, stupid but I didn't think. And now I'm going to end up in some home for it. I ask you, is that fair?'

Brendan and Marta exchanged a glance; when you put it like that, probably not. It wasn't the most opportune moment for Frank Gilroy to stick his head around the door.

'Afternoon, all. Artie, how's it going?'

Artie put on a brave face. 'Wouldn't be dead for quids, Sarge.'

'That's the spirit. Matron, I'm sorry to interrupt, it's about the fire, should I come back later? I'll have to do a report, I wondered if you'd managed to find out how it started.'

There was a beat. And then Marta shook her head. 'I'm afraid not, Sergeant.'

'An electrical fault maybe?' said Brendan. 'Isn't that usually the culprit?'

'Mm. When they start in the ceiling. But this one didn't, did it?'

'We just don't know yet, Frank. Early days.'

Frank decided he would need to have a good look round himself, it was a pity the fire brigade hadn't come in some ways. After he was gone, Artie looked at Brendan and Marta. 'Guess I owe you both a vote of thanks.'

'You do, mate. You do. Frank could have got very nasty, couldn't he, Matron?'

'Very nasty indeed. Understandably.'

Artie collapsed in a heap then. 'What's going to happen to me? What did she mean, "supervised"?' The question hung in the air. Neither Marta nor Brendan could bring themselves to answer it.

The question would, however, be decided very soon in Artie's old smoke-stained room. Fighting back tears, Pat was packing his suitcase. Strangely, she did not altogether blame Artie for what had happened, she blamed herself. She should have known her crazy idea of a holiday was never going to work; it was a silly indulgence to have even considered it. It got her dad all upset and this was the result: a near tragedy. Why couldn't she just accept her lot in life and be grateful for what she had? After all, she could be living in Africa where drought was killing millions of people.

But somehow, comparing herself to starving Africans didn't help, she just felt worse. And then, as the tears really began to flow, Terence Elliott appeared.

'Pat. Found you at last. We need to talk.'

'If it's about Dad, there's no need. As you can see, I'm taking him home.'

Terence sat down. 'I don't think that's such a good idea.'

'I don't have any choice.'

'Cavendish Lodge has a nice room, Pat. They'll hold it till tomorrow. It's a really good nursing home, the best for miles in my opinion.'

'He won't go.'

'*Artie* doesn't have any choice. You can't look after him any longer. Sixteen years is enough.'

'He's my dad. I love him, no matter awful he is.'

'Pat. This thing about going into a home. It's what he's been dreading. He's built it up in his mind until it's become his own personal nightmare. But once it's happened, I bet he becomes a new man. There are some nice people at Cavendish Lodge. People he knows. I honestly think he'd enjoy it there. And you'd get your life back. You could still go to Somers.' He paused. 'Who knows, Pat. One day you might go to Paris.'

'I'd feel so terribly selfish.'

'Yes, of course you would. But it's not selfish, it's sensible. I'm not what you'd call religious but the Bible does have some pertinent things to say now and then. You know that piece from Ecclesiastes, 'to everything a season and a time to every purpose under heaven?' Pat nodded. 'This is the season for change, Pat, this is the time. Embrace it. I'll pick you both up in the morning, that might be the best way to handle the, um, transition.'

'Thank you,' Pat said. And a whole new world opened up in front of her. She just had to break the news to Artie.

***

Shirley arrived home to find Vicky looking considerably better. She was sitting on the couch with a plate of Vegemite toast and another hot lemon drink, her third for the day. She sipped it while Shirley filled her in on the day's dramas.

'I didn't hear the fire brigade.'

'They weren't called in the end. It wasn't much of a fire, thank goodness. But everyone behaved very well. Little Silvia Popovich tried to save Birdie alone and unaided and Bill Ferguson was so impressed he proposed to her.'

'What?!'

'Something like that anyway. He did propose.'

'Fantastic! Good for Bill, I'm really pleased.'

'Yes, Esme's had to change her mind about the pickers. Sorry, *some* of the pickers.'

'And to think I slept through it all.'

'Oh, one other thing, the painters are finally out of the house in Bligh Street. Simon's moving on Saturday.'

'I thought he was charging around on horseback on Saturday.' Shirley went to answer the door and Vicky thought to herself that she might do the neighbourly thing and offer to give Simon a hand, just to show there was no ill feeling. She had changed her mind by the time Bob Hatfield came into the room.

'Bob wants to see you, darling,' Shirley said.

'I know you're not well, Vicky, stay where you are. I just wondered if I could borrow your .22.'

Vicky was a bit surprised. 'Well, I suppose so, Bob. What do you want it for?'

'Just been out at the Jones's. Molly's got this cow …'

'Oh, she rang me about it,' Shirley said. 'I told her you were sick, Vicky.'

'Yeah, well she can't get anyone else, see. And she can't do it herself and the poor thing needs to be put out of its misery.'

Vicky got up. 'I'll go, Bob. It's not your job.'

'Not yours either, when you're sick. But she did try the other vet … would it help if I drove you?'

'That'd be lovely, Bob. Thanks.'

Emily Page sealed the last of several letters, put them into one larger manila envelope and propped it on the mantelpiece. The dining-table was elegantly set, dinner for two, though no cooking smells came from the kitchen. The chef out at Hicklewhite's Winery had done her a favour and prepared a very nice meal; all she had to do was pop it into the oven to heat through. Dessert and a salad were both in the fridge. Well, she thought, she didn't indulge herself like this very often. And she could hardly get Chinese takeaway under the circumstances. She did wish Harriet could have been here; they always managed to laugh together. All the same, she thought it would be a pleasant evening.

She glanced out the window and saw Pat and Artie returning from the hospital. She was up to date on events; Terence had phoned to warn her that there could be undue shouting or crying or even the sound of glass smashing. She was to ring him if Pat needed support. Emily thought for now the warring parties did not look happy but nor did they seem about to kill each other. She hoped it stayed that way. She did not want her pleasant evening ruined.

Brendan had not been home long when Vicky and Bob arrived. Bob stayed in the ute, he didn't feel this was any of his business. He could see that Molly was still sitting beside the cow, still crying. He bet there'd been quite a bit of that in the last couple of days. Brendan had been kind. 'I'm sorry, darl. Really I am.'

'It's all my own fault.'

'It's no one's fault, Moll. It's mother nature, it's life and death.' He went to meet Vicky. 'You didn't have to come, you're sick.'

'Not as sick as the cow, Brendan.'

'Thanks, Vick.'

She just patted his shoulder and went to Molly who got up and wiped her nose.

'This is very good of you, Vicky.'

'It's fine. It's my job.'

'Could you just show me how to use the gun? I mean, where to … you know.'

'You want to do it yourself?'

'I think I should.'

'Okay.' Vicky didn't think this was a good idea at all but she loaded the .22 and handed it to Molly and showed her the spot on No-Name's temple she was to aim for. Then she moved away and left Molly alone with the little Jersey.

'I did my best No-Name. And maybe I should have let you go sooner. But you were fighting too, I know you were …' Molly tried hard but she was crying so much and her hands were shaking so much that the task she had set herself was impossible. It was Brendan who took the gun from her. 'Go inside, Moll.' She took off, running as fast as she could, trying to get into the house, to beat the crack of the rifle. She didn't make it. When it came, she stopped running. After a moment, she squared her shoulders and walked inside.

Terence having decided that Silvia could go home a day early, there was a small celebration at Bill Ferguson's farm that evening; nothing flash, just a quiet family dinner and a bottle of champagne. Alex gave his blessing to the forthcoming union and Silvia agreed that after all it was probably time that Lexy started school. They even set a date for the wedding. Then Alex diplomatically took Lexy back to the vineyard and the lovers finally had some time to themselves.

'It's all happened so quick,' Silvia said.

Bill grinned. 'One minute you're up an apple tree and now you're surrounded by cows.'

'I never thought I would be this happy again.'

'Makes two of us. Funny though – we barely know each other.'

'I know enough. Some men stop to help when you're stranded by the side of the road and some keep driving. You stopped.'

'I could have been an axe murderer,' Bill said.

'Never.' And she threw her arms around him and burst into tears again, it was a bad habit of Silvia's but Bill didn't mind in the least.

The mood at the Turner house was more funereal than celebratory. Pat was trying to make a list of things that Artie might like to take with him to Cavendish Lodge. Artie refused to participate, he said it was up to her, whatever she thought, she knew best. He just wanted to sit there quietly and enjoy his last few hours in the house which had been his home for nigh on fifty years; the house to which he had brought his bride, in which he had raised his children, and which held so many happy memories. For who knew when he would see it again?

Pat stood it for so long. 'You're talking poppycock, Dad. This isn't the house you brought Mum to, we lived in Carpenter Street for years. That's where the happy memories were, Mum was alive and you were well then. You've spent half your life here in a wheelchair.'

'Well I'll tell you one thing, girlie, there'll be no good memories of Cavendish Lodge. I know that already.'

'You don't know any such thing, you might love it. As for never seeing this place, of course I'll bring you home to visit, how many times do I have to say it?'

'It's not saying it that counts. It's doing it. Deeds not words. I bet Ralph Parker's family said they'd take him home too.'

'I'll bring you back, Dad. Often. I promise. Don't you see – these ridiculous arguments, we're driving each other insane, they're part of why we can't live together, not any more.'

'I quite enjoy a good argument.'

Pat could have killed him, there and then, but relief was in sight. One more night, she could manage one more night.

CHAPTER TWENTY-TWO

'This is splendid,' Simon said of Emily's beef bourguignon. 'I don't suppose you're going to tell me where you got it?'

'The French chef I hide in the kitchen,' Emily said.

'No, no, wait a minute … I've had this before. Gabriel made it, didn't he? Out at the winery!'

'You have a very good palate.'

'But I didn't know they did takeaway.'

'They don't.'

'Oh, I see. A favour for a special lady. Well I feel honoured to share it. But what's the occasion?'

'A private little anniversary. Just eat and enjoy. You haven't told me much about Charlie, how is he these days? Is he still working at all?'

'He was until a few months ago. Not any more.'

'Because?'

'Prostate cancer. It's not too bad. He says he'll die of old age before it gets him and he's very likely right.'

'I see.'

'I probably shouldn't have told you.'

'We're all getting old, Simon. Charlie has cancer, I have rheumatoid arthritis. But we're still alive, aren't we? And such a good life it's been. We have nothing much to complain about. You're right, Gabriel has done us proud, this really is delicious.'

And Simon, watching her eat it with such difficulty, wondered how many painkillers she'd had to take to be this bright, and marvelled again at her stoicism.

'By the way,' Emily said, 'how are thing going with Vicky Dean?'

'They're not going at all. She disapproves of me, Emily. Me and everything I stand for.'

'So you're giving up? Just like that? I am surprised. Charlie would never have given up.'

'Emily,' Simon said, just a trifle tartly, 'I am not my grandfather.'

'No and just as well for the most part. But Vicky Dean is a smart, sensible girl. Make an ideal wife for a country doctor. *If* you're going to stay in the country.'

'The jury's out on that one.'

'Don't make any rash decisions, promise me that? Rash decisions are never wise.'

'I'll remember.'

Emily insisted on champagne to go with the chocolate mousse and Simon proposed a toast to her secret anniversary, eliciting only the information that it was not connected to birthdays or weddings, which left him wondering, privately, if it might not have something to do with his grandfather. He was quite sure there had been a romance between them, maybe a real love affair, but had to accept that he would probably never know. It was very frustrating.

Simon cleared away and stacked the dishwasher and then they settled down to mahjong but Emily, he could see, was getting tired, so they only played a couple of rounds and then Simon got up to take his leave.

'It's been a lovely evening as usual. Thank you, Emily.'

'It's not a night I wanted to be alone so I'm very glad that you could come. Oh, one little favour – Pat usually posts the mail for me but what with the fire and everything … could you?' She handed him the manila envelope. 'It's all inside.'

'Of course. First thing tomorrow. 'I'll see you next week then?'

'I'll ring you. Goodbye, Simon.'

'Goodbye, Emily. Thank you again.'

Emily shut the door slowly behind him but didn't lock it. She never locked it. She knew she could need help at any time. She went back to the dining-table, where half the champagne remained undrunk because Simon was driving. There was also a carafe of water on the table. From the drawer in the sideboard Emily took out two jars of pills. The tops were loose so she could get them undone. Smiling, she sat down at the table and poured champagne. Coco, who had absented herself all evening, came and rubbed herself against Emily's legs. 'Don't you worry, my precious. You'll be taken care of. I've made arrangements.'

Simon's drive home took him past Vicky's surgery. It was now late but the light was still on. Normally Simon would have thought nothing of it but he'd heard that Vicky was home in bed sick and it seemed strange. He stopped the car, wondering if he should check it out. He sighed, whatever he did would be wrong. But after his last encounter with a drug addict – and the desperate ones had been known to go after veterinary drugs – maybe he should at least make sure it was all okay.

Vicky herself opened the door. She looked terrible. 'Oh, it's you.'

'I thought you were home in bed sick and then I saw

the light on. I just wanted to make sure you were okay.'

'No, I'm not. Bob and I were driving back from the Joneses, we had to put Molly's cow down, and there was old Mr Lawrence in the middle of the road. His dog had been run over, driver never even stopped, he was distraught ...'

'You've been operating ever since.'

Vicky nodded. 'I did manage to save him, I think. That dog's all the old bloke's got now.'

'Can I do anything?'

'Make a coffee while I clean up?'

'Sure.'

'Where have you been?'

'I had dinner with Emily Page. It was some sort of anniversary, she didn't want to be alone. Fabulous meal, Hicklewhite's prepared it for her.'

'Gosh, you were living it up.'

'It was the full bit, right down to the champagne and chocolate mousse. The more I think about it, the stranger – oh, my God, of course, and then the letters! I'm sorry, Vicky, sorry about the coffee, I've got to go, can you get home alright?'

'Yes, of course.' He almost ran out of the surgery, leaving a totally bewildered Vicky behind him.

Simon let himself into Emily's house, calling her name but of course he got no reply. It was Coco who came running to greet him, mewing anxiously. Emily was slumped over the dining-room table. She looked quite peaceful. He felt for a pulse. It was still there, weak but there. He knew she would want to be left alone. The dinner had not been to celebrate an anniversary – or if it had, that was not the only reason for it. It had been her little farewell. Why, oh why had she chosen to share it with him, to place this awful burden on his shoulders? For just a moment or two, Simon thought about letting

Emily die as she wanted to do. Peacefully, at home, with dignity. And then, because he was a young doctor who still had a very great deal to learn, he rang for an ambulance and started to apply CPR.

Marta and Simon did what had to be done to save Emily Page. They put her on IV fluids and made her as comfortable as they could. Even when she regained consciousness, she barely spoke. Her only concern was for her cat; she asked Marta to ring her cleaning lady and see if she would feed Coco. Simon sat by Emily's bed for a some time until she told him she'd prefer to be alone and then he left. He'd saved her life and lost her friendship, he understood that. He went home and opened the manila envelope. He wasn't sure what to do with the letters now, perhaps he should wait and see. They were mainly to her family; one to Harriet, one to Vicky and one, without a stamp, addressed to him. He was about to rip the envelope when he saw, written on the back, the words 'To be opened after my death.' Tempting though it was, he put it away at the back of a drawer. Emily was alive but all he felt was grief.

He talked to Terence the next morning. He did not get the comfort he was seeking.

'I think she actually hates me,' Simon said.

'And that surprises you?'

'I don't know. Why ask me there, why put me in that position?'

'You put yourself in that position, Simon.'

'Are you saying you would have let her die?'

'I wouldn't have gone back.'

'I *knew* what she was doing! It came to me with absolute clarity. I was certain. How could I not go back?'

'Your decision.'

'You think it was the wrong one.'

'Not at all. I'm saying you have to live with the consequences.'

'I was brought up to believe that life is sacred.'

'There you are then. That's your answer. For you, it was the right decision.'

Simon thought, but not for Emily, that's what he believes. In fact, Terence was wondering how to stop Simon making one of those rash decisions Emily had warned him about.

'Simon. I know you're on duty this weekend but I've got nothing planned, I don't mind covering. Why don't you go away somewhere? No, better idea, why don't you go home? Bet your mum'd love to see you.'

Terence arrived at the Turner house on time next morning, as planned. To his surprise, Artie, in his wheelchair, was waiting in the garden.

'All set to go then, Artie.'

'The fight's gone out of me, doc. Especially after what happened last night.'

'What was that, Artie? Pat, let me help.' Pat came out dragging his suitcase.

'Her next door. Carted off in an ambulance. I suppose she's gone, has she? Heart, was it?'

'Nothing like that, Artie. Mrs Page is doing fine. She'll just be in hospital for a day or two.'

'Oh, thank goodness,' said Pat. 'I did hope it was nothing serious.'

'No, absolutely not,' said Terence, thinking well at least that was true of the outcome. 'Shall we go?'

'Do I have any choice?' said Artie.

'Not this time, Dad. You're going to Cavendish Lodge and I'm going to Somers. And we're both going to have a really nice time.'

Terence almost clapped. The worm, he thought, has most assuredly turned.

***

Vicky went out to check Bill's cow and was able to offer her congratulations to the happy couple. It was amazing, she thought, how people – and animals too – bloomed with the promise of happiness. Silvia looked like a schoolgirl. Vicky asked about wedding dates and found that they wanted to get married as soon as possible, though Silvia would first have to find something to wear.

'I've told her it doesn't matter,' Bill said, 'she'll look beautiful no matter what.' But Vicky, being a girl, understood the problem. And being Vicky, she thought she might also have a solution which she duly passed on. And then Lexy told her how he was starting school tomorrow while Tiffany was still there to look out for him. He was a bit worried though, because Tiffany thought he ought to talk about his cyst for show and tell. What did Vicky think? And Vicky agreed with Tiff, it was just the best, the grossest idea ever. (Which turned out to be true and made Lexy a bit of a star on his very first day.)

Vicky then went to see Molly. It wasn't a visit she was looking forward to and she was glad to see that Bob had been there already with a back hoe and poor No-Name had been given a decent burial. Molly insisted on making tea. 'I know what you're going to say, Vicky, and you're quite right, of course you are. I've got to toughen up. And I will. I am. I behaved very badly over that cow and it won't happen again.'

'Molly. Please. Don't be too hard on yourself.'

'I left her lying there for hours. And then I couldn't even put her out of her misery myself. It was a terrible thing to do.'

'Even if you'd had a gun, or you could have given her an injection or something, it's never easy ending an animal's life. I've had to do it hundreds of times and I hate it. It's just that sometimes not to end it is worse.'

'I know that now.'

Vicky smiled. 'She had a good couple of days before the end. She would have thought she was in heaven out here. Mash and molasses.'

'You think?'

'You bet. Listen. Is there any chance you might have time to make a wedding dress?'

'Who for? Oh – I know! Lexy's mum. Silvia. How soon does she need it?'

'About a month?'

'Gosh. If it's not too elaborate.'

'I said you might be happy to take a nice little Holstein poddy calf for payment.'

Even Brendan thought that was a good deal.

On Friday afternoon, Terence called to see Emily at the hospital. 'A couple of bits of good news.'

'That makes a change.'

'I got out to Cavendish Lodge today. Artie's started a euchre club. He's cheating outrageously and winning hands down.'

'Are they ready to kill him?'

'No, no, they all cheat. He seems to be settling in really well. So Pat's off in the morning. Oh, and guess who's taking her to the station?'

Emily sighed. 'Frank Gilroy. That's not good news.'

'Shirley arranged it, of course.'

'Of course. A hopeless cause, she's like King Canute. Trying to turn back the tide of Frank's devotion.'

'I'm glad you can still joke, Emily.'

'I'm weeping inside, Terence. What was the other good news?'

'You can go home tomorrow.'

'I thought you'd want to lock me in a psychiatric ward.'

'We'll get you more help. You can afford it. I'll give

you more pain killers.'

'I am grateful for your trust. I won't put you in a difficult situation.'

'I know.'

Despite the promises made, Terence hoped he was doing the right thing. He found Marta in her office. 'Are you riding in the morning, by any chance?'

'I was planning to.'

'Why don't you ride out to the vineyard? I'll have breakfast ready.'

'A ride with a destination. How lovely.'

No one had told Vicky about the near-tragic events of the night before. Shirley was tempted but was not in the habit of breaching patient confidentiality. At the hospital, a cone of silence came down on such things, as it should. Vicky, however, had been somewhat put out by Simon's abrupt departure. She needed to know, since it doubtless involved his obsession with Emily Page, what had brought it on. She was getting worried about Simon. Well, she would have been worried if she cared. So she called at his unit and found him throwing a few things into a bag.

'Getting ready for the big move, then? I actually came to see if you wanted any help. I mean, I thought you were playing polo originally, but Mum told me the house was ready.'

'I've given up polo. And I'm going to Sydney.'

Vicky was shocked on all counts. 'Sydney? Not permanently?'

'No, of course not. For the weekend.'

'Why?'

'Why? Because I made a terrible mistake, Victoria. One with disastrous consequences. That is, I don't think I had any choice in the matter. But everyone else seems to think I did the wrong thing. Especially the person most – most intimately involved.' He stopped, he was close to breaking down. It suddenly hit Vicky what this was all about, why he had dashed off so suddenly.

'Did Emily try to kill herself last night?'

'Yes.'

'And you went back and stopped her.'

'Yes.'

'Oh, Simon,' Vicky said sadly, 'why?'

Simon just stared at her. 'That's why I'm going home,' he said. 'To be with people who think like I do for a while. Who understand why I had to do what I did.'

Vicky nodded. Then she gave him a hug. 'Drive carefully,' she said.

'It can't last, can it?' Terence leaned back in his chair, lapping up the morning sunshine.'

'They're predicting storms by this afternoon,' Marta said. 'All the farmers will complain. Too much rain or not enough.'

'Careful, I'm a farmer now.'

'A vigneron.'

'That's Alex. He's a marvel.'

'You were lucky to find him.'

'I didn't. It was fate. Shirley saw it in the tea leaves.'

'I wonder what else she saw and hasn't told us about.' There was a long look between them. 'Weren't you going to Melbourne this weekend?'

'I was but Simon needed a break. I'll go to Melbourne next week. Everything's alright for the moment.' She just nodded, content with that. Terence was glad she wasn't the sort of woman who demanded lengthy explanations.

'Do you think Simon will be alright?' she asked.

'It'll take him a while to get over this but I think he will. I hope so. He'll be a damn good doctor one day.'

'He's a good doctor now, Terence.'

'Yes, of course he is, but don't you dare tell him that. What a pity I'm on duty, we could have had some champagne.'

'You could bring it round this evening. I'll cook.'

'I do like a woman who picks up a hint.'

EPILOGUE

Simon's grandfather, Charles Bowen, still liked to sail and on the Sunday morning they went out on Sydney Harbour. It was a picture postcard day, the water crowded with leisure craft, ferries darting back and forth, and a liner disgorging rich American tourists at Circular Quay. Above it all the bridge stood aloof, busy with trains and thousands of cars, the footpaths surprisingly crowded with pedestrians making the long walk across.

There was just enough breeze to keep the sailors busy for an hour or two. Finally they anchored in their favourite bay and talked about life and death and doctoring. Charlie, who had seen a great deal more of the last two especially than he hoped Simon ever would, was able to offer some words of wisdom. But he felt the mood had become a little melancholy and when Simon finally asked him for the truth about Emily Page he was not at first inclined to give it. But he changed his mind. He knew he was running out of time and he felt it would be a shame to take the story to his grave. It never occurred to him that Emily would object.

'I asked her to marry me,' he said. 'And she turned me down. Not while the war was on, she said. She thought we had a job to do, we should be concentrating on that. I thought it was just an excuse, that she didn't care for me enough. Took it as a personal rebuff, fool that I was.'

'But she did care,' Simon said.

'I met her by accident a couple of months after VP day. Some cocktail party. She said "Ask me again, Charlie." But of course it was too late.'

'You were married.'

Charlie nodded.

'I'm going to get in touch with her grandchildren,' Simon said. 'They don't go to visit her very often. I don't think they know how lucky they are. I don't think they know what they're missing out on.'

'I loved your grandmother, Simon. But I always knew what I'd missed out on. One of a kind, Emily Page.' He pulled out some sandwiches and they munched on them for a while in companionable silence.

'That girl you seemed keen on last time we spoke, the vet, what was her name?'

'Victoria.'

'Yes, what's happened to her.'

'I saw her on Friday.'

'Oh?'

'She told me to drive carefully.'

'Doesn't sound terribly romantic.'

'She didn't like me much for a while. But I think we might be friends again. That's all, though. Just friends.'

A COUNTRY PRACTICE BOOK 3

Continuing the story of the country folk of Wandin Valley ... Enjoy a preview of the first chapter of the next book in the *A Country Practice* series of novels.

The night was cold and bright, so clear the stars seemed to hang close enough for plucking; so clear that sounds, even small sounds – the slam of a car door, the creak of a gate, the crunch of hooves on frosted earth – echoed across the valley.

It was no night – or rather morning, for it was now after four – to be sitting in an outdoor dunny but that is where Molly Jones found herself, wondering why she had ever left Adelaide and the civilized comforts it had to offer. She took care not to shine her torch into dark corners, for the outhouse was home to any number of small creatures, most of them possessed of eight spindly legs. Business finished, Molly stepped out again into the night and felt the cold wrap itself around her. In spite of it, she did take a moment to glance at the magnificent sky; admiring the Southern Cross in all its splendour, she failed to see the fox slinking towards her chicken yard.

Brendan Jones, who was waiting on the edge of sleep for the piercing shriek of the alarm clock, felt Molly slide back into bed beside him. She rubbed Brendan's leg with an icy toe.

'Bren?'

'Mm?'

'We have got to get an indoor loo.'

'Sure, darl. One day.' Sleep crept up on him again. Blessed sleep.

'Bren?'

'Mm?'

'There's something I forgot to tell you last night.'

'Oh yeah.' Brendan fought his way out of the fog and came to his senses. They told him to be wary.

'I had a call from Bianca yesterday.'

'Bianca?'

'Forbes-Hamilton. She was one of my best friends at school.'

Well of course she was, Brendan thought. Molly had attended a ladies' college where names like Forbes-Hamilton abounded.

'And what's Bianca up to?'

'She's coming to visit.' And then it all came out in a rush, so Brendan couldn't get a word in edgeways. Bianca hadn't seen Molly in ages. She was a model, just back from a *gruelling* overseas assignment and she needed a bit of R and R in the country. Brendan would just love her, she was such fun. She was arriving tomorrow. Wasn't that terrific?

Fortunately, Brendan was prevented from voicing his true feelings about Bianca's imminent arrival by another, altogether different sound. It was being made by a lot of terrified chooks and only one thing could be causing it. Brendan was out of bed in one swift movement and Bianca was forgotten.

'Damn that bastard fox!' he yelled, dragging on boots and a battered old dressing-gown.

Molly was also struggling to throw off the doona. 'My chooks,' she said. 'I'll go.'

'Don't be silly. Time I got up anyway.' The alarm shrilled to emphasise the point as he charged off towards the chook yard in the pre-dawn light, wishing he had more than a pitchfork to brandish at the intruder, wishing he had the rifle he'd wanted to buy but Molly wouldn't have a bar of. He thought how ridiculous he must look and almost laughed out loud. Maybe he and the fox could have a good laugh together and come to some agreement.

No chance of that. It was still too dark for Brendan to see how the fox had gained access to the yard; that it had done so was not in doubt. Three of the terrified birds jostled and squawked together on their roost. The rest of Molly's girls as she liked to call them, the other four, lay dead on the ground with their heads bitten off. Brendan just stood and stared at them. He was a nurse. He was used to death. What he couldn't cope with was wanton destruction. He'd seen enough of it working in emergency in big city hospitals; here it was in microcosm. And yes, perhaps it was just a few hens he was looking at, but they were Molly's hens, part of her small farm family. Brendan would have understood if the fox had taken one to feed *its* family but this slaughter – this went against all the laws of nature. He was angry. They needed to get a dog, he thought. A very large dog. But first he had to go and ruin Molly's day before it had even started.

Foxes were not a problem for Terence Elliott. He grew grapes on a small vineyard he'd acquired just a few months ago. The predators here were the silvereyes, which descended from the heavens when the grapes were fat with juice, and stuck their sharp little beaks into them and sucked them dry. Right now, however, the silvereyes were off on their winter migration and Terence himself, nursing a cup of hot coffee and gazing at the rows of sleeping vines, felt a rare sense of contentment. He was grateful for such moments; they did not come so often as they once had. He could not put his finger on the reason for it; why his life had lately seemed a little out of kilter, but there was no denying it did. It wasn't his work, he derived great satisfaction from being a country GP, and the vineyard had given him a hobby he enjoyed. But he still felt that life was somehow passing him by, that it needed a cataclysmic jolt to set it off in a new direction. So he savoured these few minutes when all seemed well with the world.

People had said he was mad to buy Eldershaw Estate but he'd fallen in love with the place just as its previous owner had predicted; the fact that he'd also kept his sanity was largely due to the man beside him. 'You've done a fantastic job with the pruning, Alex,' he said.

'To prune is good.' Alex's English was heavily accented, he had come to Australia from Serbia after the war. 'To cut away the dead and make room for new growth – very satisfying.'

'More like very hard work.'

'Next week I like to start trimming the roots. Is okay?'

'The roots?' Terence clearly had no idea what he was on about.

'The ones that grow sideways. We cut them off. This encourage the ones that go down?'

'Oh. Oh, I *see*. Yes, that makes sense. I learn something every day from you, Alex.'

'To learn how to grow the best grapes – this takes time, Dr. Elliott.'

'I never doubted that for a minute. But please – tell me if you need more help. Don't overdo it. We can't have you exhausted for this wedding.'

Alex smiled. 'My part is easy, only to give the bride away. I just hope she stays well now.'

'She's made a very good recovery. She's going to be fine.' Silvia, the bride in question, had recently contracted measles, of all things, and the wedding had been delayed for some weeks. But it would take place in a fortnight and the nice thing was, Terence thought, that not a person in Wandin Valley didn't wish the couple well. The Popoviches – Alex, his widowed daughter-in-law Silvia and her young son – had arrived in town with the fruit-pickers. But fate had intervened, Silvia had met Bill Ferguson, a local dairy-farmer – and the rest was history. Terence drained his coffee mug.

'You not only know about vines, Alex, you make a damn fine coffee. Thank you. And now I'd better go and visit a few patients, I suppose. Though I think I'd rather potter round here all day.'

Alex just smiled. He didn't believe that for a minute. Terence Elliott would always be a doctor first. The vineyard was just a minor passion.

Marta Kurtesz, matron at the local hospital, was also out and about indulging a passion that crisp winter morning. She'd been riding her horse, The General, for over an hour and was just thinking, like Terence, that her time was probably up. She should head back to the stables, where her car was parked, then home to change. She wasn't due at work until ten but the hospital was chronically understaffed and she intended to go in early. She might, with any luck, at least catch up on the paperwork. She enjoyed a last canter through the state forest, splashing through the icy water of a small creek, then came to the road. Two kilometres more and she was about to turn into the stables when she saw a dog lying not far from the gate. She dismounted and went to look.

It was a kelpie, no stray this but some farmer's working dog.

He wasn't dead but looked close to it. Marta acted quickly. She left the dog, rode fast up the long drive into the stables and called to Jean, the owner, who'd been expecting her. Marta explained the situation and Jean promised to look after The General and give him a good rub down. She also found an old blanket.

'Here,' she said, 'wrap him in this. Was he hit by a car, do you think?'

'Hard to say. It doesn't look like that.'

'Well keep me posted.'

'I will. Thanks for taking care of The General.'

'Not a problem.'

Marta collected her station wagon and picked up the dog on her way out. She wrapped him up, laid him gently on the back seat and headed for the veterinary clinic, praying that Vicky Dean would be on duty and not out attending the birth of some prize heifer.

Vicky's mother, Sister Shirley Dean, was definitely on duty, having just opened the Wandin Valley Clinic and found, to her dismay, that two windows had been broken and the place was like an icebox. Dr Simon Bowen arrived soon after and since the windows were at opposite ends of the clinic and the damage was almost certainly not accidental, pressed her to ring Sergeant Frank Gilroy. Which Shirley did, albeit reluctantly. The good sergeant adored Shirley, indeed his adoration was such that half the town expected a wedding before the year was out. But that was the half that didn't know Shirley as well as they liked to think.

She had no intention whatsoever of becoming a policeman's wife. None. (Frank, on the other hand, believing in the attraction of opposites, had no doubt at all that he would eventually succeed in his suit.) Shirley hung up the phone. 'Five minutes. He says there's been a spate of vandalism.'

'Kids bored out of their brains no doubt,' said Simon. 'Nothing to do in winter. Maybe you should ring a glazier as well, Shirl. It's positively Arctic in here. Can I help you clean up the glass?'

'Haven't you got house calls to make?'

'Only two. You sweet-talk the glass man.' Simon got a dustpan and brush from the small kitchen and then stopped. 'Oh. Maybe Frank won't want us disturbing the crime scene.'

Shirley giggled. 'Thank God you thought of that. No, of course we mustn't, he'd have a fit. Go and make your calls, Simon, I'll manage.' Simon collected a few things from his surgery and left. Shirley got a promise from the glazier to come as a matter of urgency later in the morning. Then a surprisingly officious Sergeant Gilroy arrived, closely followed by Esme Watson who was Terence Elliott's first patient.

'Goodness gracious, Shirley, whatever happened?'

'That's what I'm here to find out, Miss Watson, if you wouldn't mind keeping out of the way?' Frank gave her a glacial smile and she took a seat, much put out. 'Now, Shirley – just the two windows?'

'That's right. I walked in this morning and found them broken. As you see.'

'When was this exactly?'

'Not long before I rang you. Maybe fifteen minutes before.'

'You say you "walked in". Was the door unlocked, then?'

'Not at all. It was completely locked as usual. I had to use my key.'

Frank was prowling round by now, taking notes. 'I see. So no sign of forced entry.'

'No sign of any entry, Frank. Just the broken windows.'

'And I don't suppose you saw anyone?'

'No, Frank. Not a soul. Not until Simon arrived.'

'And where is Dr Bowen now?'

'He's making house calls, Frank. Or do you think he's gone off to smash up someone's property?'

Frank was just a little hurt, he felt her sarcasm was uncalled for. He said stiffly, 'I just wondered if he might have anything to add. As I mentioned on the phone, there's been quite a lot of vandalism. It's my job to find the culprit before it escalates into something serious.'

Shirley felt a little abashed. Poor Frank, he was just doing his duty, he didn't deserve her sharp tongue. 'I'm sure Simon doesn't know any more than I do. He thought it was probably kids, bored with nothing to do in the winter.'

'And he's probably right. But boredom's no excuse, is it?'

'In my day,' said Esme, unable to keep quiet a moment longer, 'we found more than enough to occupy ourselves. There was always the library.'

'You need to know how to read, Esme. Ah, here's Dr. Elliott.'

'Heavens, said Terence, 'have we been burgled?'

'Nothing so exciting,' said Shirley. 'Just a random act of wanton stupidity, wouldn't you agree, Sergeant?'

There was nothing random about the act which had brought the kelpie Marta found to Vicky's surgery. The dog had been poisoned. Marta watched, and helped where she could, while Vicky gave the animal an injection and even started to insert a stomach pump. But the stethoscope gave no sign of a heartbeat and nor could she find a pulse in the femoral artery. She began to pump the dog's lungs with both hands and kept it up for a long time until she was exhausted. Then she looked at Marta and shook her head.

'He's gone, Marta.'

'Poor thing. Who would do that, Vicky? Poison a beautiful dog?'

'A farmer, maybe. Trying to protect his animals.'

'But a kelpie?'

'I know. Unlikely, but not impossible, that it might attack something. I need to do an autopsy, find out what sort of poison was used, if I can get the owner's permission.' She looked at the tag on the dog's collar. 'Which shouldn't be a problem.'

'Who did he belong to?'

'Fiona Collins. She breeds coloured sheep for their wool. For weaving, you know? She rang me this morning to tell me her dog was missing.'

'And the day started so well. I had a wonderful ride …'

'At least you found Rusty and brought him in. Fiona can take him home if she wants to, bury him on the farm. She'll be grateful, Marta.'

It was not much consolation but Marta knew they had both done all they could. She still had to go home herself and change into her uniform and get to the hospital. She was going to be late. She borrowed Vicky's phone to ring Brendan and warn him.

At the hospital Brendan hung up and thought he should have warned Vicky that she was likely to get a visit from a rather overwrought Molly, but he didn't ring back. He'd left his wife talking somewhat manically about baits and traps for the fox and wanting to know what was legal. But perhaps she'd calmed down by now. Sister Judy Loveday came in.

'Where's Matron?'

'Running late. She's been trying to save a poisoned dog.'

'Any luck?'

'No.'

'I wonder what it did.'

'Sorry?'

'The dog. For someone to poison it.'

'Maybe it was accidental.'

'Mm.' Clearly, Judy didn't think so. 'Mrs Horley's demanding to see Doc Elliott.'

'She already has, he came in early.'

'You and I know that, but how to convince her? Will you have a go?'

'If you make me a coffee,' Brendan said. But both Mrs Horley and the coffee had to wait.

Out in the corridor, a voice called, 'Someone, please …'

Brendan and Judy both rushed out. An extremely agitated mother was supporting a girl of about nine. The latter was wheezing badly, barely able to breathe, and the mother's panic wasn't helping matters. Brendan, who knew all there was to know about asthma, picked the girl up and took her into the nearest examination cubicle while Judy went to call Terence Elliott. From the mother's reaction, it might as well have been a kidnap attempt. She went from panic-stricken to totally hysterical.

'What are you doing! She's got asthma! It's bad, it's the worst attack she's ever had, that's why I came here!'

'I know it's asthma, Mrs –?'

'Burns. This is Camilla.'

'Mrs. Burns. So why don't you just wait there and let me treat your daughter?' Brendan tried, gently, to close the door on Mrs Burns but she wasn't having a bar of it.

'You can't lock me out, I'm her mother, I've got all her medication! I know what she needs!'

'Mrs. Burns, please. Could you try to calm down? This a hospital, we treat children with asthma all the time, we know what your daughter needs too. Calm and quiet, first up.'

Judy returned. 'Doctor's on his way.'

Mrs Burns looked at Brendan, horrified anew. 'You're not even a doctor?'

'I'm a nurse.'

'Then we're waiting for the doctor.'

'Mummy?' Camilla was distressed, sobbing, her breathing worse, if anything.

'I'm here, darling. I'm here.'

'I'm sorry, but we can't wait for anyone, Mrs. Burns. This is an emergency. Now would you please go outside?'

'I can't leave her alone with strangers! She'll just get more upset!'

Brendan had had enough. 'I said go, Mrs. Burns. Now. Just wait outside and let us do our job.' Mrs Burns stood there a moment, looking at her daughter's outstretched arms. And then at Brendan's implacable face. She wavered and Brendan saw her waver and took her by the shoulders and steered her out the door and shut it firmly behind her.

A Country Practice Book 3 is published in paperback and as an ebook from Amazon in early 2016.

Read more about the series at
www.acountrypractice.info

ABOUT THE AUTHOR

Judith Colquhoun was born in Queensland and grew up in Sydney. She studied production at the National Institute of Dramatic Art and soon after graduating, love and a job at the ABC took her to Melbourne. There she learnt to drink coffee, wear black and follow St Kilda in the AFL. Later, she lived in London for a time, spent many years in country Victoria and long enough in Italy to fall in love with the Mezzogiorno. She is now back in Melbourne and may even stay there.

She started writing when she was six and from the age of twenty-three has always earned her living from it in one way or another. She was a scriptwriter for far too long, writing countless hours of television for many of Australia's most popular shows. Her output included one hundred episodes of *A Country Practice*.

Judith has worked as an editor and script producer and in Italy was a script consultant on the serial *Un Posto Al Sole*. She has won five Awgie Awards and in 2007 was made a Life Member of the Australian Writers' Guild.

In 2009 she finally gave up scriptwriting to attempt a novel. *Thicker Than Water*, which is largely set in southern Italy, was published in 2014. It was Highly Commended in the Fellowship of Australian Writers 2014 National Literary Awards.

Judith is married with two children and three grandchildren.

Printed in Great Britain
by Amazon

24148801R00131